ZOMBIE HAVEN

The Fence Book II

By C.G. Buswell

Copyright © C.G. BUSWELL LTD 2023
All Rights Reserved.

www.cgbuswell.com

This is a work of fiction, and any character that bears a resemblance to anyone living or dead is a coincidence. The author imagines the events and places, and bears no similarities to actual events or places.

For Angela and Izzy of Hidden Wounds, thank you for soothing my fractured mind.

Chapter 1	1
Chapter 2	15
Chapter 3	22
Chapter 4	28
Chapter 5	42
Chapter 6	52
Chapter 7	64
Chapter 8	72
Chapter 9	79
Chapter 10	85
Chapter 11	97
Chapter 12	107
Chapter 13	118
Chapter 14	126
Chapter 15	135
Chapter 16	146
Chapter 17	164
Chapter 18	170
Chapter 19	179
Chapter 20	189
Chapter 21	199
Chapter 22	211
Chapter 23	215
Chapter 24	222
Chapter 25	226
Chapter 26	243
Chapter 27	249
Chapter 28	259
Chapter 29	266
Author's Note:	271

Chapter 1

The bullet thudded into the shoulder of the running man. He had dried blood crusting on his mouth, down his neck, and onto his flapping shirt. It exited after ricocheting off his clavicle, causing a huge hole to burst from his back. He didn't feel a thing. Nor did the smaller woman, behind him, as it burst through her face, the heavy 8.59mm calibre bullet exploding her features like a burst tomato. Her all-in-one waterproof jacket, reaching down to her ankles, didn't protect her clothing from the gushing torrents of blood that poured from her writhing arteries and veins as they danced and made her muscles contort and twist.

Both undead were victims of the Russian plane that had flown overhead yesterday, spilling a strange yellow smoke, turning Aberdeen and the surrounding Aberdeenshire into a death zone. Those affected by the chemicals had turned feral upon each other, craving the blood of those few lucky enough to survive. The couple, united in death, took another faltering step, then dropped to a merciful release. As an act of irony, the man twisted as he fell and lay prone on his back as if awaiting the delivery of the woman. She obliged and fell on top of him, her mushy neck nuzzling into his unfeeling face, giving the appearance of a last embrace.

'Fuck me!' exclaimed Imogen Pritchard as she watched through the Schmidt and Bender eye scope of her new favourite weapon, the L115A3 sniper rifle, given to her at the newly constructed fence near the border of the county of Angus. 'That's fucking fantastic.' Her smile exposed her missing teeth. The start of black decay in those few remaining gave away her years of drug dependence and personal neglect.

Her companion, Flight Sergeant Jason Harper, put his hand to his mouth and gave a few dry heaves. His shoulders and back arched from the floor of their battered Land Rover, and his free hand grasped the lip of the lowered tailgate. 'They were people,' he sighed as he dropped his other hand from viewing through the single sight of his spotter lens, the Mark 4 Tactical Spotting Scope.

'Not anymore, Cowboy! If you are going to spew, crank your head over to the gravel, and watch out for Sabre, I don't want any vomit on his fur.'

As if in expectation, their furry friend, a huge German Shepherd dog, began sniffing around the weeds beneath the tailgate the unlikely couple was spread on.

'Let's find your next target. Try not to snatch at the trigger. You went wide of the heart,' advised Jason. He looked to Sabre, 'Lie down,' he ordered. 'I don't want you shaking the tailgate and making Imo miss.'

The dog instantly hunched down and spread his long legs, awaiting his next command.

'I was aiming between his eyes. I wanted to see his head erupt. But two in one shot, how about that? Got to be a record!'

Jason shook his head in distraction. 'I'm afraid not. A British sniper in Afghanistan took out eight towel heads with one shot. It's thought his shot hit a suicide vest, and it was straight to Allah for them.'

Imogen muttered incoherently under her breath as she took aim, from the top car park, down to the hillside path and up to the ruined castle that stood proudly on a high, rugged hill, its rear and side sprouting on mighty solid rocks. The North Sea battered impotently against the solid rocks below, as it had done over the centuries. Sheets of white and blue water tried to cascade the sheer walls and then ebbed back to the sea in a hasty retreat. There was fleeting movement around the mixture of roofless buildings, except for the modern-day visitor centre. The armed couple didn't need to travel the 800 metres down the path and then up the steep incline to get to this ancient monument. Their dull black and green weapon's bullets travelled within two seconds; the fist-sized Lapua Magnum bullet fired effortlessly from the sniper rifle. The enhanced suppressor, at the tip of the muzzle, created little noise, nor flash, designed not to give away their position. The colonel, who had left them a couple of kitbags crammed with gear and an assortment of weapons in the back of the Land Rover, had thought of everything.

'Slow your breathing down. We are trained to not feel the emotion. Each target we aim at isn't a human with a family. We are taught to see them as only a target.'

'So why do you vomit every time you kill?' mocked Imogen.

Jason's face reddened. 'It's not always easy.'

'How many have you killed? In the military, I mean, before we went all zombified.'

He sighed. 'People, they were people. Please try to remember that. I didn't keep score. Some lads did, but I couldn't. It didn't seem right, and I wanted to forget that I'd created orphans, widows and grieving mums, dads, siblings.' His voice tailed off as his eyes narrowed and creases ridged his forehead. It took a few seconds for him to come back to the present, and he knew she'd be keeping a tally. He had lost count of the enemy he'd killed in the Royal Air Force and now of the undead.

Imogen let off another round, not waiting for orders from Jason. He hadn't even time to raise his spotter's scope.

A woman dressed in a black skirt, tartan waistcoat and white blouse fell to the ground as crimson spread throughout her torso.

'She won't be giving any more guided tours to her bus passengers.'

Jason clenched his teeth as he looked down the lens at Dunnottar Castle, the pride of Stonehaven. He felt the warm rush of bile come up his oesophagus and battled to prevent it from reaching the back of his throat. He gave a few swallows before saying, 'Movement to the left, among the smaller buildings, near to the edge.'

'Got him.' She took a few slow breaths as she tracked the running man, dressed in the dark green polo shirt of Dunecht Estate, saw the red eyes as he turned, then gently squeezed the trigger. He fell, tumbled towards the grass, and rolled a few feet towards the incline.

'Was he infected? I couldn't see blood around his mouth.' Jason gripped the tailgate, not because of the rising bile but because he so desperately wanted to take back some living people to the colonel. Perhaps then he would allow him to see his wife, Pippa.

'Relax Flight Sergeant Harper,' she mocked. Just because you've suddenly been re-enlisted, it doesn't give you the right to order me around.

'It does,' he retorted, then relaxed his grip. 'Not that I can do that. You are your own woman. You are doing well.'

She gave a toothless grin. 'Thanks, Cowboy. Will I get a special badge? Like the one the Royal Air Force gave you?'

He laughed, despite the situation. 'You can have mine. All those computer games you played in prison have made you a better shot than me.'

She lowered her rifle and twisted to face him. 'For real? Cool!' She raised her arm and put out a palm and he reluctantly high-fived her.

Jason turned back to the edifice of the hulking castle. A teenager was running down the hill, weaving around the path that embraced the contour of the looming rock. She stumbled over a body, fell, and immediately set upon its neck, appearing to snuggle into it. 'She's feeding. Drop her.'

Imogen turned back to her weapon, tracked along the winding path, found her target, aligned her weapon's crosshairs, and gently squeezed the trigger. There was a slight recoil into her shoulder as the gun, resting on its built-in Harris Tripod, spat out its bullet, like a male orgasm, and gave immediate relief to the infected girl. Her head snapped back, leaving a trail of brain, blood, and bone upon the path.

'Perfect. For once, there are no strong winds to factor in.' He tapped the small cylinder like apparatus that was on top and to the left of the barrel. 'We'll go through that dial later and how you make adjustments for the wind speed and direction.'

Imogen rolled her eyes as she drew back the black, round bolt. A brass case flew to her right, and another round was chambered from the five-round magazine. She knew he was itching to mansplain. He'd already talked at length when she naively asked why each magazine only held five bullets. She had let him drone on about heavy calibre and long lengths. It had all sounded penile to her. All she cared about was the killing and how much fun it brought her. She tracked along the sturdy walls of the taller, three-storied building.

'We've a live one!' exclaimed Jason, his words spoken in a rush. 'Look to where the windows would have been on the upper floor of the second building from the front. It's been a few years since Pippa and me were there. I seem to recall the floors had been lost to the weather over time and never restored. It's a woman. She must have climbed up the stones somehow. She's dangling over the window ledge, looking behind her. She's screaming. I can't see what at. It must be an infected person. Oh my God!' he cried out. 'She's being dragged back. The fall will kill her.'

Imogen pursed her lips as she watched the woman disappear. 'Let's hope so. It'll be quicker for her.' She lowered her scope, but the thick stone walls of the building did not reveal their secrets. 'Want to mount up and take a closer look?'

'No. There's nothing we can do. Let's give it a few minutes looking for new targets, then make our way into town.' He nodded towards the two large coaches in the car park. These buses had taken tourists from the local cruise ships, docked in Dundee or nearby Aberdeen, whose ports had been recently developed further to host larger ships. It had been a boon for the local tourist attractions. The cruise ship staff had furnished each passenger with a long waterproof jacket, the material as thin as a black rubbish bag, but their material had been see-through. Great at keeping their charges dry and easily disposed of once the rain subsided, as it had now. Imogen and Jason were bone dry, shooting at each infected tourist and several staff members of the Dunecht Estates who owned this top attraction.

Sabre, still obediently beneath the tailgate, gave a low growl.

'Is this sniper rifle any good in a close firefight?' asked Imogen, almost casually.

'No, it's better at taking down targets about six hundred metres away, maybe up to two thousand, given the right weather conditions. In Afghanistan, a kill was recorded at-' began Jason.

'So, no use against them,' revealed Imogen with more urgency as she leapt to her feet, allowing the sniper rifle to remain on the floor of the Land Rover. She turned and swung her SA80 rifle from its sling on her back and quickly shouldered its stock to her shoulder and let off several carefully aimed shots into a crowd of pack-a-mac wearing tourists of mixed races, each with the same collective intent – to kill Jason and Imogen.

'Bollocks!' rasped Jason as he got to his feet, grabbing his rifle from the floor. He whistled to Sabre, 'Up boy. Attack!'

A ball of dark brown and black fur scuttled from beneath the tailgate and ran around the side of the vehicle. With a few bounds from his long limbs, he was on the first of the infected. His teeth were clenched firmly on a plastic-coated arm, wrenching it clean off the shoulder with its fierce grip. As the unfeeling victim fell, Sabre released his grip and bit at its neck. Imogen no longer had to worry about keeping its fur clean. It was now sleek with fresh blood.

Worried he'd hit the dog, Jason flicked his catch to a single shot and took careful aim at the front runners and watched as each fell, causing those behind to stumble or trip. Jason took two quick steps forward, to the roof of the cabin of the Land Rover and quickly laid his weapon down for support and began shooting at the heads of the infected. He took no satisfaction with each clean headshot. As each head snapped back, he moved immediately on to the next target, knowing that from this range, he'd have made an immediate kill. His weapon gave the dead-man's click as the bolt ran home and he expertly ejected his magazine, allowing it to fall, and quickly inserted a fresh one, pulling it out deftly from his chest rig which stored all sorts of equipment and was strapped to his torso. He pulled back the cocking mechanism and began firing into the thinning crowd.

Sabre moved onto another fresh victim, having shaken the life out of his first. He went barrelling into the crowd, knocking several of the runners to their feet. He felled a fourth by clamping down onto its dainty ankle, exposed beneath the hem of the rain garment. He soon found flesh and began shaking his large head. The body jerked about, as if given a prolonged electric shock.

Imogen walked the length and breadth of the back of the Land Rover shooting at the faster runners who had broken free from the felled bodies. She shot each swiftly through their heads. Soon the gravel car park was awash with fresh blood, tiny bone fractures and the dull grey colour of brain. Piles of bodies laid about resembling a one-sided battlefield. A portly man, dressed in a white shirt and black trousers was her latest victim. She guessed this was the driver and the red shiny staining on his black tie gave away that he'd fed recently. Imogen felled him with one clean shot through his eye.

Jason quickly wiped beads of sweat from his brow that were threatening to drip down to his eyes and obscure his sight. He then aimed for a fresh target but found none. Corpses were all around him, the only movement was from Sabre who was shaking at the face of his latest victim. 'That'll do, boy. Heel,' he commanded as he turned his head to the left, leant over the vehicle, and vomited.

Above the sound of Jason's retching, the couple heard a pump-action shotgun being loaded and a yell of, 'Drop your weapons.'

Chapter 2

'Who the fuck are you?' demanded Imogen as she aimed her rifle in the stranger's direction. Sabre sprang up to the Land Rover, ready to defend his pack. He sat growling at the stranger, yearning for the 'Attack!' command.

The man's aim did not falter, but he relaxed his stance. 'You can call me Tex.'

Imogen looked down at his portly belly, which bulged over his fouled checked shirt and lay heavily on his mud-splattered jeans. Her eyes rolled when she saw his cowboy boots. Then she glanced up at his head, knowing it would be there. She wasn't disappointed. He wore a wide-brimmed cowboy hat, like JR Ewing from Dallas. 'Just what we need,' she muttered. She sidled along to Jason and patted him on his back as he dry-heaved. 'Hey, Cowboy, you've got competition!' Sabre stopped his growling as he sensed the tension amongst the trio dissipate.

Jason stood up and snatched up his rifle, ready to point at the stranger.

'Easy fella.' The man tore off his tinted sunglasses. 'See, no red eyes. Not like that lot.' He pointed to the piles of corpses. 'Nice shooting, just like a turkey shoot.' He looked at their weapons and chest rigs, but squinted when he saw they wore jeans and t-shirts beneath their combat chest rigs. 'You the military, then?'

Jason nodded while Imogen declared, 'Am I fuck! No one orders me around.'

The Stetson hat nodded up and down slowly while the eyes of the stranger looked her over. 'I can belief that, Missy.'

'Cut the American crap. I can hear the Aberdeen accent beneath it, Tex. How did you survive?'

'I've no idea what's been happening. All I know is I came out of my escape room. I like to spend a night or two down there, now, and again, and when I climbed back out, all these lunatics with red eyes are wandering about trying to kill me. I tried dialling 999 but all the phones are down. My landline and mobile.' He nodded to Jason, 'So, military man, what's been happening?'

'Your escape room? Like an enclosed room with its own ventilation system?' asked Jason.

The man beamed and tried to suck in his belly. 'The finest in Aberdeenshire. Other preppers come from far and wide to visit. I've a bed, stacks of food and water, cooking area, chemical toilet and all the comforts of home like a generator, TV, and DVD player.'

'And probably loads of porn, the dirty bastard,' muttered Imogen.

Tex waved his shotgun in her direction. 'Say something, Missy?'

Her knuckles went white against the barrel of her rifle. 'Like a dungeon, Tex?'

'That's right, down a few ladders. Dug it myself. That's the joy of living in an isolated farmhouse, no nosey parker to tell on the Council if you dig without planning permission.'

'The smoke won't have penetrated that far down then,' offered Jason.

'Smoke?' questioned Tex, lowering his weapon now.

'A jet unleashed a chemical weapon.' Jason turned and pointed to the corpses and put his hand to his mouth, fighting down a rush of bile. He gave a small burp.

'Goddamned Russians?' Tex interjected, squinting his eyes into the skies.

'That's right. I saw one of our planes head after it, but the damage had been done. We've been tasked with finding survivors or kill the infected. There's no cure.'

'Bastards. As if Ukraine wasn't enough. That's because of all the weapons we've been supplying to that country. This is payback.' He looked around him, back to the main road, around the nearby thicket of trees and then towards the path leading to the castle. 'Where's the rest of you?'

'It's just us,' beamed Imogen proudly, showing the stranger her few remaining teeth.

'Just for this area? You've more patrols out, surely? The plane must have infected a wide area?'

'No, just us for the entire region. We've been fenced off. Contractors and the military have built a big fence to keep the infected in,' sighed Jason, wondering if he'd ever get through the defences to get to his wife in Dundee.

'No way, you'll never cover it all.'

Jason nodded. 'The military doesn't want to risk getting their own killed. I guess the infected will eventually turn on each other and do the killing for them.' He looked behind him. 'And with our help.'

'You volunteer or something?'

'That's right, I guess you could say we are expendable.'

Imogen chirped in, remembering a series of films she'd watched in prison for her latest string of thefts. 'We are The Expendables!'

Jason rolled his eyes.

'Who did you piss off?' asked Tex.

'It's a long story. Ask the colonel when you see him at the fence.' Jason pointed south. 'Head off on the A90 and you'll come to it. Drive slowly, the road has obstacles. Then you'll be freed.' He brought his hand to his mouth again as he remembered the mound of corpses gunned down by the heavy calibre rounds from the helicopter earlier in the day.

'No chance. I'm not leaving until I've bagged a few zombies myself.' He scratched at his groin, 'And maybe have fun with the better-looking ones.'

Imogen and Jason both crinkled their noses at this disgusting comment and left it hanging in the air between them, like a foul smell.

Tex pointed his gun at the driver's side of the battered Land Rover. 'I'm guessing Mike didn't make it?'

Jason and Imogen looked at each other and shrugged.

'He owned the farm next to me. That's his Landie.'

'Ah,' replied Jason. 'I guess he didn't. Unless he was evacuated to safety. We were allocated this, under orders. We only stopped here on the way into town as we wanted to find somewhere quiet to look over the gear we were issued.'

Tex looked around the pile of corpses. 'I'd hate to see your busy place.'

Jason grimaced. 'We got side-tracked when we saw movement running from the castle. We couldn't save anyone. I doubt we'll find many survivors. Not everyone will have worn masks like we had on or a self-contained basement like you.'

'Or a creepy dungeon,' muttered Imogen.

A ringing phone interrupted the awkward silence. The couple looked at Tex in anticipation of him taking out a mobile. 'How come you've got a signal?' demanded Jason. His thoughts turned straight to his wife. He jumped down from the back of the Land Rover and began walking to Tex with purpose, but stopped as soon as he saw Tex's pointing finger. The ringing was coming from the kitbag they'd thrown into the corner of the rear of the Land Rover.

Chapter 3

Jason jumped deftly back onto the open rear of the Land Rover and scrambled for the kitbag where the noise was coming from. He pulled out clothing and boxes of field rations, a cooker and two gas canisters and boxes of ammunition. He was more careful when he spotted a plain brown box with the label 'Grenades' and, despite the insistent ringing, laid it carefully to one side.

Imogen tore open a ration pack, rummaged inside, and pulled out a packet of biscuits. A black nose was instantly snuffling the wrapper and was rewarded with a plain-looking biscuit. Imogen joined Sabre in a mid-afternoon snack. She didn't bother offering any to Tex.

The phone continued its ringing, rising in volume above the crunching and munching noises. Finally, Jason located it at the bottom of the kitbag, nestled between layers of socks. He couldn't help but count over a dozen pairs. The colonel knew it was a long mission and had equipped them accordingly. Jason had also spotted winter clothing and his heart sank.

He pulled out the phone and saw the word 'Alpha' flashing on the screen. He pressed the accept button and put the phone to his ear.

'Took your fucking time.'

'I didn't know we had this in our kit.'

'You'll address me as sir,' growled the caller

Jason recognised the voice as belonging to the colonel.

'Of course, sir, sorry, sir. Hello Colonel-' he left the sentence hanging, hoping to get a surname. His distant memory was telling him he knew the officer, but didn't recall his name. He knew it was related to the fatal mission in Yemen.

'Never mind the small talk. Get to your mission. I want the friendlies back in one piece. This is your chance at redemption.'

'I want to speak to my wife,' demanded Jason.

'No chance. I'm the one giving orders, Flight Sergeant Harper. Don't ever stay your finger on a trigger again. Get to your co-ordinates. There is a map in the other kitbag. It's civilian, so you'll need grid references, no more RAF talk, I'm Army.'

'What grid references?'

The line went dead. Then a message immediately pinged on the phone, displaying a grid reference. Jason memorised it and began dialling a number, but the phone wouldn't work. He slipped it in his pocket, anyway.

'That fucker from the watchtower?' asked Imogen, no longer smiling.

'Yes. We've got to find a map in the other bag.'

Imogen gave the rest of her biscuit to an eager Sabre. 'How does he know where we are?'

'Through the phone. But even if we threw it away, I figure there will be tracking bugs somewhere in the vehicle and in the kit. Probably the weapons as well because he knows we'll never be far from them. Even if we took them apart and cleaned and oiled them, we'd probably never find them, as they could be tiny.'

'Clever fuckers,' whistled Imogen through clenched teeth. She reached into her chest rig and fingered a small medicine bottle.

'Take some, I think you'll need it.'

Imogen turned her back on Tex and quickly took out a bottle, poured some into its cap, and necked the green liquid. Her tongue darted out, and she licked at the precious Methadone drops within. Then, just as quickly, she furtively put it away in her nearest pouch.

Tex squinted at her, trying to see around her slim figure. He gave up and then gave a long, salacious leer at her bottom. It looked pert in her figure-hugging jeans.

Jason clocked his obscene look and moved to block his sight. He quickly unlaced his blood-encrusted boots and took them off, along with his socks and then moved the mobile to his chest rig pocket, stripped down, revealing his lithe, muscled torso and strong biceps, unfurled a combat shirt and trousers and donned them. He scooped up a lanyard with a blue piece of material on in. Embroidered on it were three chevrons and a crown. He instinctively put it around his neck and tucked it deep beneath the olive-green t-shirt. He noted there were no dog tags with his name, rank, serial number, and blood group.

No Medical Emergency Response Team would be pumping blood into him if he got wounded. They were on their own. He kicked his soiled clothing aside and began rummaging in the other kitbag for the map. He passed Imogen a pair of combat trousers. He knew they would fit her perfectly. The damned colonel would have seen to that. Looking towards Tex, he ordered, 'Turn around while she changes.'

'You sure know how to spoil a man's fun.'

Jason ignored his comment and waited to see the stranger turn before he spoke softly to Imogen. 'We'd better look the part. Survivors will be more trusting of us if we look like soldiers.' He squatted down, back turned to her, and put on a pair of black combat boots and set about lacing them while she changed. Jason didn't take his eyes off Tex, not for a moment.

The colonel watched the flashing circle on the screen as he took a large swig of his coffee. He grimaced at the cold, bitter taste, though he was really pulling a face at having to trust Harper. He'd wanted to lead a squadron of the elite in putting down the so-called zombies. He knew his crack troops would soon put them out of their misery and find survivors. Instead, he had his own orders, to not risk anymore troops, because soon, they might be needed to launch a ground attack on Russian soil, depending on how the peace negotiations were going. The politicians feared another chemical attack, one from drones or missiles launched from afar. The jet in Aberdeen had been a mere show of strength. Instead, his troops, along with all available personnel from the Royal Navy, Royal Air Force and the Army, had worked through the night alongside the Royal Engineers to erect an enclosure, penning in the infected, and the survivors along with them. Harper had at least given them a glimmer of hope. If he was up to the job.

Chapter 4

Jason stared at the cabin by the lower car park, squinting his eyes against the sun, trying to focus from this distance.

'Hankering after a coffee?' questioned Imogen. 'I could murder a full-bodied, real beans coffee. None of this instant shit we've had to make. I'm a flat white girl. I bet you are a black, large, no sugar. Nice and strong, like your biceps!' she quipped.

Jason nodded absently, not taking his eyes off the Portakabin type hut, not even when Imogen playfully felt his arm muscles.

She gave up and looked in the direction he was staring. 'Something up?'

'Yeah. When we got here, that small window, with the mesh, was closed. I remember looking around the hut, yearning for a hot drink, thinking of an easy way in. Now it's open.'

'Well spotted, Cowboy. They teach you that in the military?' She cupped her hands around her eyes and mimicked looking around.

He nodded again, eyes intent on the snack shack. He raised his SA80. 'Tex, take the path to the left. Imo, take the right. I'll go straight ahead. Cover me while I jump over the wall. You whistle for Sabre, Imo.' Jason didn't wait for their acknowledgment. He was back in military mode and giving the orders. Jumping onto the wall, he looked down at the drop, dangled his legs over, and eased himself down to the next car park level. The grass cushioned his landing, and he crouched to one knee, eyes down to his rifle sight. His weapon tracked the length of the snack outlet. From the corner of his eyes, he waited for Tex and Imogen to approach, and then he moved between the picnic benches. The only sounds came from the local seagull colony in the distance and the nearby sparrows who were missing the crumbs from the sandwiches and rolls. He banged on the back door with his fist. Several sparrows and a blackbird flew out from the nearby bushes.

A rumble echoed around the interior of the coffee shack and a mug fell on the floor, the clatter and smashed crockery alerting the trio to someone inside.

'It's safe to come out,' shouted Jason. 'Open the door and come out, but raise your hands and keep your eyes open.'

'Who are you? Why has everyone gone crazy?' questioned a frantic female voice.

'It's safe. We are the military. Open the back door and step outside.'

A creaking noise revealed the door opening a fraction. 'Let's see your identification?'

Jason rolled his eyes, took out his wallet, and flashed his defence discount card. He hoped the union jack insignia would convince the lady. He made a mental note to ask the colonel for his RAF ID card back again.

The door opened further to reveal a woman in her twenties, wearing a cotton apron with pockets in the front. An order pad and pen were jutting out. Her hair was tied back in a bun and she wore a branded t-shirt which matched the logo on the sign he'd spotted on the front of the cabin earlier. She glimpsed at the plastic card. She laughed. 'That's just a discount card.

My brother has one of those. He always buys the KFC because he gets ten per cent off.'

Jason grinned at her. 'You're clearly not infected. Come on out. Let's get you to safety.'

'What do you mean by infected? Is that why people have been attacking each other? Is it some sort of virus?'

'No. The Russians attacked this area with chemicals. It's turned people against each other. Were you wearing a mask yesterday?'

'Oh!' she exclaimed. 'I was, now I think about it. Sorry, I've been in there all night. I'm tired. People have been trying to get in. I always wear a mask when I'm topping up the hot chocolate powder. It makes me breathless otherwise. I have mild asthma. One minute I'm serving my regular. He comes every day to sit at the bench he donated in memory of his daughter.' She pointed to the sloping grass. 'He drinks her favourite drink and has a black pudding roll for his breakfast. With a dollop of brown sauce. Then, quite out of character, he leant over the till area and grabbed me. I panicked and closed the shutters on him. I think I may have broken his fingers. But he was attacking me.'

'You did the right thing,' reassured Jason.

'Since then, there have been bangs and thuds against the shutters and doors. I was too frightened to step outside. I tried dialling for help, but my phone wouldn't work. I fell asleep on the floor at one point, but woke up cold. Then I heard your firing and muffled conversations. I opened the window to hear you better.'

'This is going to sound strange, but I need to get you to safety. Can you drive?'

'Yes, but my boyfriend dropped me off. He was supposed to pick me up last evening.'

'Imo, Tex, come on round. We have a friendly.' Jason walked to the nearest corpse, one they'd shot through the head when they first arrived and were looking for a good lying up position. He noticed its bruised fingers as he delved into its pockets and removed a bunch of keys. Attached to it was a black plastic fob with several buttons. He depressed the one that showed an open door. Looking around the car park, he spotted a silver hatchback whose lights and indicator flashed twice. Pointing, he told her, 'Get in there.' He handed her the keys. 'Don't look down or around you. It's not a pretty sight. Drive to Dundee, don't stop for anyone. Slow down when you near a large fence stretching over the dual carriageway. There may be a big ditch and a broken-down articulated lorry before it. Halt when you are near them. You may have to weave around piles of bodies,' he warned.

Her eyes widened. 'What have you had to do?'

'It's best you don't ask. Just get going. Stay safe. Don't be alarmed at the sight of lots of people in military uniform. They are there to help you.'

'What about my boyfriend?' she asked, smoothing down her apron.

'I'm sorry. He may have got to safety, or he may have,' he struggled to find the best word to finish his sentence but gave up and left it hanging.

She bit her lip and took the keys from him.

Tex walked around from the left. 'I'll help you there, Missy. I'll keep you safe until you drive off.' He licked his lips as he stared at her breasts.

She shuddered. Ignoring him, she strode off to the car.

Imogen nodded to Jason and followed them, eyes on Tex.

Jason slowly entered the hut, SA80 held at the ready. He narrowed his eyes at the gloomy interior. 'I wish I'd been issued a head torch,' he muttered. As his sight adjusted to the dark, he looked longingly at the coffee machine and made do with stuffing his empty pouches with a selection of wrapped fruitcake and flapjacks.

Soft padded feet followed him in and a sniffing sound filled the shack. Sabre was rewarded with a giant shortbread biscuit thrown down by his paws. It vanished in one bite.

The young woman reversed quickly. She hadn't checked her mirrors and was shocked when the car lurched to its side. She crunched the gears into first, not daring to check what she'd run over. Then she gunned the engine and turned out of the car park and gave a scream at the pile of bodies she had to manoeuvre around as she crested the hill and turned left. She didn't look back.

Tex was shaking his head, his enormous hat surfed along with the movement. 'Shame, she was well fit.' He watched as the car disappeared.

'Fucking pervert,' muttered Imogen as she aimed her rifle at the bulky figure of the man. A hand gently lowered the muzzle, and she turned to see Jason munching on something.

'No coffee?'

'Power is still off. Help yourself to snacks, though. Some are super soft. Don't forget to leave a tip!'

She grinned her toothless smile. 'Cool.' Sabre followed her into the cabin.

Tex made to follow, but a restraining hand held him back. 'Don't get in our way,' hissed Jason with narrowed eyes.

Tex took several steps back, gulping as he moved.

'Sabre, up.' Imogen patted the lowered tailgate, and the dog bounded up, gave the soiled clothing a good sniff, and coiled himself around the discarded t-shirts. As he lay on the floor of the Land Rover, he rested his chin on a pair of jeans.

'You can travel in the back with Sabre,' ordered Jason to Tex.

Tex looked at Sabre as the dog gave a low growl. 'No chance. I've got my own transport. I'm all equipped.' He pointed to a shiny pickup truck parked on the nearby road. Its roof was adorned with several additional large spotlights.

'Probably full of perverted ropes, handcuffs and gags,' whispered Imogen.

'Yeah, I don't get a good feeling from this one, either' muttered Jason as he reached over to tickle Sabre's ear. He avoided his chin, where the infected blood was still damp on his fur. In a louder voice, he said, 'Okay, we'll meet at the harbour. I'd like to let Sabre swim in the sea to wash off the blood.'

Tex took a step back. 'The disease, or whatever it is, doesn't get transmitted by blood then?'

Jason and Imogen shook their heads, and Imogen showed her blood-filled palms to Tex. The dried red was in sharp contrast to the earthy staining around her fingernails and digits. Washing wasn't top of her priorities. 'No worries there. I've eaten from these hands. The chemicals were short acting, but it's going to take a while to end all the infected.'

Tex walked closer to the Land Rover. 'What are your names? You haven't introduced yourselves.'

'No, we haven't, have we,' challenged Imogen, not liking the way this man leered at her.

Tex broke the stare as Jason spoke. 'Jason, and that's Imogen.'

'Imo?' asked Tex, with a slight tilt of his head.

'Only to my friends,' she insisted.

Tex walked up to the tailgate. 'I'm sure we'll be that, Imo.' He went to stroke Sabre, but returned his hand back to his shotgun as the dog let off a deep growl.

'Where did you get a shotgun like that? I can't imagine Police Scotland would allow farmers to wield such a man-stopper,' asked Jason as he checked it over.

The stranger yielded and came closer. 'They don't. Let's just say I have had some eastern Europeans come and pick my strawberries. They smuggled in some choice pieces for my personal use. It's handy living so close to a harbour.'

Jason let the comment slide, but wondered how this man had survived and hadn't bothered to save any of his workers. He wondered if they'd had a helping hand to no longer be of help to the farmer. Infected or otherwise.

'Want to ride with me, M-' Tex corrected himself in time.

Jason gripped his rifle that bit tighter. 'Imogen will be driving me.'

'No offence, partner,' nodded Tex, placing a broad smile on his face. 'We can always take turns later. To drive I mean.' He walked away, chuckling as he went to his truck.

Imogen raised her rifle, but the barrel was gently pushed aside again.

'Leave it. The colonel might have eyes in the skies.'

Imogen looked up. 'Drones, you mean?'

Jason nodded.

'Cool!' She stuck her middle finger in the air, breaking the tension between the couple with laughter, despite the carnage that had occurred minutes earlier.

Sabre stood up, gave himself a shake to rid himself of his nervous energy and drying blood, and then laid back on his self-proclaimed bedding.

'Let's get going. Need directions?' asked Jason as he remembered an earlier quip from Imogen that she'd never been to Stonehaven.

'No, you're all right. I'll take this road here and then turn right into the harbour area. Left would bring me to the Market Square of old Stonie.'

Jason's eyes squinted at the mention of the local nickname for the town and watched with twinkling humour as she leapt down from the back and secured the tailgate. He noted splatters of blood from the dog's shaking had soiled her otherwise clean combat trousers. 'I thought you've never been here.'

Her face reddened as she explained, 'Only for work, a few years ago.'

A lightbulb went off in Jason's head as his eyes widened in realisation. 'By work, you mean?'

'Okay. Stop judging. I was pick-pocketing. A girl's got to eat.'

Jason thought, 'And take drugs,' but kept this to himself. Aloud, he said, 'Ever been there during Hogmanay? To see the fireballs?'

Imogen looked down at her feet. 'Yes, but I didn't take in the sights. I was working.'

'Working the crowds?'

'I guess so.'

'Probably when I had my wallet pinched!'

She kicked up some imaginary dust at her feet. 'Maybe.'

He leaned over and gave her a playful nudge with his elbow. 'Not that it matters anymore. Money has no meaning now, not for us.'

She grinned. 'All the shops are free now!'

He laughed as he walked to the passenger seat.

Imogen walked around the other side, but not before she knelt by a grey, bloodied, outstretched hand, and wriggled free a diamond engagement ring. Some habits were just too hard to kick, she thought.

Chapter 5

'Creepy fucker, isn't he?' laughed Imogen, as she crunched the gears of the protesting Land Rover.

'Yes,' agreed Jason as he leaned forward and peered in the mirrors. 'Let's see what he's like in a firefight. It's strange that he wants to stay with us, rather than get to safety.'

'We'll get you through that fence, I promise.'

Jason turned to her. 'I know. You're quite the resourceful girl, even if your aim is a bit off on The Long.'

'Cheeky fucker. What's The Long?' She waited out for the mansplaining and wasn't left hanging.

'It's what we snipers call the L115A3.'

Imogen rolled her eyes. 'It's all too penile. Can't you afford sports cars? Mind you, that's easier than remembering all those numbers and letters.'

Jason thought back to the grid reference, glanced at the map on his lap, and then looked back to Sabre, fast asleep in the back. He really needed a dip in the sea. 'Take a big breath in and hold it before firing The

Long. It'll improve your shot as you won't be moving. Head shots would be kinder. They were people once.' He looked down at his new combat boots. 'Twenty-three,' he whispered. 'I can still see their faces.'

A room full of desert camouflaged combat trousers and immaculately creased shirt wearing soldiers were peering into several monitors and laptops scattered around a dimly lit room. Apart from the faint clicks of computer mice every few seconds, the room was silent. Each man and woman were studying several arrays of live video feeds. Some screens were divided into four and even eight clips, allowing the viewer to scrutinise the movements of the infected. Most of the clips were in colour, but some of the older systems they were hacking into were in black and white. Some feeds looked like they were coming from front door cameras of civilian houses, while others appeared more like professional systems from shopping centres and service stations, another from a corridor within a hotel.

The colonel paced the small strip of flooring behind one row of monitors and then eyed up the other three ranks. Movement caught his attention, and he walked swiftly around for a closer look. A dashcam, looking like it came through a bus windscreen, was showing a Toyota pickup truck following a battered Land Rover. 'How sweet. They've found a friend. Follow them,' he barked to the technician, who was furiously clicking away at his mouse. He didn't turn to acknowledge his superior, but spoke, as if speaking into the small microphone that was hooked down from his headphones, 'Yes, sir.'

The colonel hovered silently behind him. He wasn't a man who easily trusted others to follow his orders, not in this outfit. He thought back to his days with the Special Air Service. Now that was a regiment you could trust to do the job. He began mumbling out loud, 'Why didn't they send that clown to safety? He's got his own transport. It looks like it could get through any obstacle. Our engineers have cleared the A90. He'd have a clear run.'

The technician remained silent. He, and the others in the room, were used to their officer's incoherent mumblings and knew when to remain silent. They'd all heard the rumours about this one.

A wood pigeon flew over the Land Rover, like a bomber from World War Two, its plump breasts reminiscent of the aircraft's bays packed with bombs. This one didn't release any of its cargo, but sailed on past, reminding the duo that life goes on, for some. It flew into the nearby row of tall trees.

Imogen banked the Land Rover to the right to avoid a barrier on the road. 'What the fuck is that?' She pointed to an open-air row of carriages, each able to sit four people and each attached to the other by metal rope-like tight attachments. At the head was a sole carriage, with only one seat. A man, slumped over the steering wheel, wore what looked like an old-fashioned train driver's uniform. His cap was at a jaunty angle but his red stained uniform gave away his deathly fate.

'I haven't seen that for years. I didn't know it was still running. That's the Stonehaven Land Train,' beamed Jason. He looked over the light blue and white painted engine section that replicated an old steam engine. The vehicle number plate below the furnace gave away that this was powered by electric or petrol. The wheel rims had been blocked over with wood and painted to look like mighty pistons. The roof canopy on the second carriage had been ripped apart and several bodies had been flung aside when it had driven into the side of the road. It looked like they'd been fed upon. With a sad note in his cracking voice, he explained, 'It took tourists from the town centre to the castle and back to the caravan park and open-air swimming pool. There were lots of stops for them. It runs throughout the summer months.' He faltered, 'Or it did.'

Imogen slowed the vehicle and pulled over to the side, about ten metres from the Land Train, just before the woods gave way to rows of Victorian looking housing. She ran out and jumped in by Sabre, who opened one sleepy eye, then nestled further into the discarded clothes and continued sleeping. Imogen pushed his matted fur to one side and slipped out a long, camouflaged holdall and unzipped it and laid the contents over the roof of the cabin. She swiftly pulled out the tripod and checked the cartridge casing was secure, then pulled back the bolt lever and loaded a deadly bullet. She aimed The Long down the road.

Jason followed her, lifting his arm, palm outwards, to Tex, in the universal stop sign. He waited to see he got the message before turning back to the road. 'What have you seen?'

'There's a zombie, about a dozen houses up, by the shop.'

Jason didn't have the heart to correct her about the infected. Instead, he pulled up the pair of binoculars that had been dangling around his neck as Imogen sighted her rifle and steadied her breathing. She had been listening to him.

'That's not a shop,' began Jason. He stopped when he heard the muzzle unleash its deadly load. Then he ducked as a fireball detonated up ahead. His retinas registering the immediate orange flash, and then the yellow and black after-effects just before he instinctively closed his eyes. His free hand was raised to cover them. When he opened them, a second later, he saw Imogen leaping and dancing around the equipment stored in the back of the Land Rover. Sabre was up and prancing with her.

A victim, engulfed in flames, staggering across the road, took several faltering steps, despite the flames eating away at his flesh, and silently collapsed as he reached the far pavement, still alight. There was no further movement from him.

Seconds later, Jason's hearing returned. The blast, even from afar, had momentarily deafened him. He could now hear the whoops of delight coming from Imogen.

'Did you see that? That got rid of that fucker!'

'And any survivors hiding there?' he rebuked. He looked through his binoculars, scanning the burning fuel station. The blast had ripped open the canopy that sheltered the pumps and had obliterated a vehicle, the fuel dispensers, and about half of the station building. The shrapnel would have been devastating to anyone within about twenty metres. Flames were still sparking up. He could make out chunks of burnt flesh, peppered with holes, scattered along the forecourt. 'Was that necessary?'

Imogen shrugged. 'It's the only way I'll beat that sniper's record. There were several infected milling about the cars. I aimed for the fuel pump and it ripped right through the metal. Fuck me, but I almost got blinded!' She looked through the eye scope for a closer inspection of her handiwork.

Jason shook his head. The binoculars moved left and right with him. He was regretting his mansplaining now.

The camera operator leapt back in her seat and an oath erupted from her, breaking the silence in the room. She was drawn to the burning man and couldn't take her eyes off the sight; despite the horrors she was witnessing. The man next to her gave her screen a quick look and a brief smile cracked his lips as he saw the flames and settling debris. They'd be gossiping about this in the canteen tonight, while the colonel was in his lonely room, eating by himself again. There were bets about how many kills Imogen can tally up above Jason's. Few were rooting for the Flight Sergeant.

Tex jumped out of his Toyota and ran up to Imogen. He stopped at the closed tailgate, sensibly deciding that he couldn't jump the height. 'Nice one. They've been overcharging me for years!' He put up his hand for a high-five.

Imogen ignored his filthy hand as she returned to scanning ahead through her eye scope. 'All clear.'

'You just going to leave me hanging, Imo?'

'Looks like it.' Imogen glanced up and down at him and asked curtly, 'What's your real name?'

Tex slowly removed his hand from the air and let it dangle by his side. 'Bob,' he reluctantly answered.

'You even been to Texas?'

He shook his head.

'Figured.' She looked at his shotgun. 'You know how to shoot straight with that?'

'I'm getting better.'

'Then make sure you learn quick and stay out of my way.' She nodded to Jason. 'He's kept me alive so far. We don't need you getting in our way. This is a two-person mission.' She pointed back to the way they'd driven. 'The border is that way, do one.'

'Not till I've had me some fun!' he beamed.

She turned around and began stowing the sniper rifle, her hand dancing between the task and her Glock 19 holstered to her chest rig.

Chapter 6

A hand banged on the window of a nearby nineteenth century townhouse, palm to the glass. It slid down the pane and then was immediately snatched away as two infected women fed, dragging the man to the floor, away from the bay window. The sight was lost to Jason, Imogen, and Tex as they waited for the burning fuel to recede.

Huge plumes of smoke gushed up the air and sat above the town like dark rain clouds.

'That should announce our arrival,' chastised Jason.

Imogen grinned, admiring her handiwork from behind the driver's seat.

Jason looked down at her tactical vest to the squat round black singular object with a ring, like those around keys, and a flat top with a metal lever which hugged the contours of the object. 'You found the grenades then?'

'Oh yes!'

'These have a three second fuse delay before they go bang. No smoke, just lethal force. Maybe give me some warning before pulling the pin. I couldn't find ear defenders in our kit, but I'll be able to duck and put my fingers in my ears.'

She giggled like a girl asked on her first date. 'I will. That colonel doesn't expect us to survive, does he? Otherwise, he'd have given us ear defenders. He doesn't care if we go deaf.'

Jason turned, as if to see the winter weather gear stowed in the back. 'No. But we will. Survive, I mean, won't we? We've got this far.'

She beamed, half in thanks for not mansplaining on how to throw a grenade, the other half knowing that he had her back. She looked in the rear-view mirror and squinted, not sure of their new friend. She turned the key to the ignition and set off, slowly at first, taking the time to rubberneck at her handiwork at the smouldering garage.

The phone in Jason's pocket rang shrilly and Jason looked at the screen. A scowl passed over his face. He had hoped it may have been Pippa. He pressed the screen to accept the call.

'Tell her to stop fucking around, get to the map reference, now.' The colonel hung up.

'That was short and sweet,' quipped Imogen.

'He called to admire your shooting skills,' lied Jason.

Imogen smiled her toothless grin as she drove the familiar route towards the harbour. She'd spent a morning and afternoon walking this way, several years ago, familiarising herself with the route. But, more importantly, the back alleys and small streets where she could run in the dark and get pursuers lost, should her pick-pocketing be felt or seen. But she never was, well, only once, but the girls in prison had soon taught her to be lighter to the touch. Since her release, she spent every Hogmanay here, blending in with the crowds, appearing to be enjoying the spectacle of the fireballs. Only she wasn't watching the men and women swinging their metal balls with encased bundles set alight, like some Mediaeval weapon. She was going from person to person, relieving them of wallets, purses, and mobile phones. The drunker they were, the better. She'd even got some watches and gold bangles one year. She smiled at the memory. Then her face darkened.

Jason glanced at where she was looking. 'Christ!' he exclaimed. A woman was hanging out of the third floor, granite blocked, white-framed window. Her long hair dangled down like a short rope. Strands gently fluttered in the breeze. Her arms flopped inside the windowpane, pinning her into position. A red streak filled the single-paned glass of the old-fashioned school. Small bodies littered the concrete playground. 'Let's not go in there. I can't face such horrors.'

Imogen whistled through her teeth. 'I don't fancy it either. It looks like all the children and their teachers are dead. It's not on our mission brief. This isn't the grid reference.'

They both looked away and stared ahead in silence.

As they reached the narrower streets of the oldest part of this traditional fishing town, she nudged Jason. 'Did you enjoy the fireball celebrations, despite losing your wallet?' She wanted both their minds off the ghastly sights they'd just seen.

'I was relieved of it, but yes. Pippa loves all that tradition, and the fireworks display. We managed to get to the harbour in time to see the fireballs thrown into the sea after midnight.'

'I used to watch the fire dancers at the Market Square. The way they twirled their batons while they were alight was magical and entrancing. I got lost in them.'

'During your tea break, was it?' jibed Jason.

'Ha! Yes, it's thirsty work stealing from the rich!'

'You've no morals, have you?'

'None whatsoever and they've got us this far.'

He smiled.

She appeared to suck in her lips as she squeezed their vehicle past a mobile home, one of the large American-style ones that dominated the old street. It was a narrow fit. She pulled up next to the jetty, which ran parallel with the sandy beach. As she wrenched back the handbrake, Sabre gave a bark of excited anticipation.

Jason swiftly exited the vehicle, SA80 rifle at the ready. He scanned the quayside, along the row of old buildings, part pub, hotel, and restaurant. The row of cottages adjacent to them was now holiday lets and Airbnb's. He whistled for Sabre to jump down and then pointed to the sea. 'Go play, boy!' Dog and man ran to the water's edge, Jason stopping at the gentle ebb and flow of water while the dog ran straight in, taking in playful mouthfuls of salty water and spitting them straight out. He jumped over the gently lapping tide and then back into the water and then, when he ran out of submerged rocks and sand to step on, he swam in circles, with only his wet head peeking out of the sea. He left a trail of dark red in the water as he followed the direction Jason was walking.

Imogen joined them, SA80 slung around her back, pistol in hand. She didn't wait to see if Tex had got his wide Toyota truck through the narrow gap. She doubted it. She looked at how content Jason appeared to be as he took time to stroll by the water's edge, admiring Sabre's strong swimming. But then he broke into a run while frantically shouting at Sabre to follow him.

Imogen whipped round, expecting to see danger. There was nothing and no one there. She turned back to Jason, laughing, 'What's rattled your cage?'

'Take cover,' he commanded as he ran past her, dragging her along with him. He pushed her down behind a delivery van, parked outside the inn, an old tavern, now a modern restaurant with rooms above. 'Can't you hear it?'

She looked around her and then at the clouds above as he pointed his finger skywards. She tried to see through the smoke that had followed them down from the garage in the gentle breeze. Then she made out a whistling noise, then suddenly there was a mighty explosion that rocked the van, forcing them precariously towards the white-washed wall of the building. The van settled as a shower of sand, mixed with fragments of rocks and seashells, burst down upon them.

Jason wished they'd been issued with some helmets as a stone bounced off his scalp. He stood up, rubbing his head and offering his other hand to Imogen to signal all was clear. She took it, rose, then brushed herself down.

His phone rang.

'That was a show of our strength and ability. Now get on to the job at hand. Get in there and find him alive, and bring him to me. Room three.'

Imogen walked around the van and ignored Tex, who was flat out on the road, hugging the tarmac. There was a crater on the beach, as if a World War One artillery shell had landed there and carved out a new rock pool for the tourists to catch crabs in.

Jason joined her. 'It was a missile from a drone.'

She looked up at the sky, eyes squinting.

'You'll never see it.'

'But you heard it?'

'Oh, yes. Once heard, never forgotten. We've got to go in there.' He pointed to the pub entrance. 'There will be a doorway at the back to get to the bedrooms. We've to go to room three. I'll need you to cover me.' He pointed to their left. 'That's another entrance to the hotel rooms for the guests. It saves them from going through the pub. But I think the staff entrance may have been less used. We should be safer this way.'

She nodded; her pistol was gripped tight. She pointed it at the prone Tex. 'What about him?'

'Leave him. He's no use to us. Let's complete this part of the mission and await fresh instructions.'

As they passed the horizontal, quivering Tex, he shouted out, 'Is it safe?'

Imogen winked at Jason. 'No, another is on its way. Best stay down.'

They quietly tiptoed past him, and Jason patted his trousers, beckoning Sabre to follow them. He entered the building first. He ignored the long bar with its shiny pumps for draft ale and rows upon rows of whisky bottles, behind where the bar staff would have attended to their thirsty customers. With weapon barrel pointed ahead and his eyes down the weapon's sights, he slowly made his way to a doorway behind the bar and pointed his weapon up the stairs. He waited a second or two before ascending slowly. Imogen followed, her pistol aimed behind her, Sabre close by her heels. Silence greeted them, save for the gentle crunch of broken glass under their stealthy footsteps.

There were two bodies at the top of the stairs. The smell and presence of flies told him they had been long dead, perhaps some of the first victims to the infected. Jason's boots felt sticky underfoot with the thick layer of dried blood on the deep carpets. He had to pull each foot off with a concerted effort. He didn't bother going into the first two rooms, but stopped at the third. He nodded to Imogen and turned the door. It moved about an inch and then he felt resistance. He pushed further and heard a dull thud as the door gave way, causing him to fall through the doorway, pushing the door open as he righted himself. His hand went to his mouth as he began dry heaving.

On the floor were four men, each with a clean slit across their throats. Their mouths were caked in blood. Not theirs, for they had bled out towards their chests or around their shoulders as they fell. They had been infected. Their bodies were in the space between the bedside cabinet and the bed, made as if for a new guest, sheets tight, duvet smoothed as crease-free as possible with a row of three cushions propped by the plump pillows. A thin counterpane at the foot of the bed matched the nautical blue of the cushions. No blood had stained the crisp linen. At the foot of the bed was a woman, a neat hole through her forehead, her hands were bloodied and there were patches of skin under her fingernails. Sitting in the chair, head lolled back, was a slim man, throat hacked out, face deeply scratched. Beneath his outstretched hand was a Sig Sauer P226 handgun, a slimmer looking pistol than the one Imogen held as she followed Jason in. On the man's upper arm was a tattoo, a dagger thrust through a pair of wings. Beneath his chair was a dropped, bloodied commando knife.

By the window, with fine views of the stunning harbour and peaceful water, was an undisturbed table with a notepad. Jason glanced at it and noted the jotted down timings. He glimpsed at the small tripod with the binoculars and built-in camera. He didn't need to inspect it to know it would have built-in infrared night-vision.

Jason took out the phone, flicked through a few icons on the screen, found the camera app, and began taking photos of the notepad and the man's corpse. He typed, 'Sorry. He's been dead at least 12 hours.' He sent this and the images to the only number in the Contacts. He turned to Imogen. 'Let's go downstairs. I can do with a drink.'

Chapter 7

The door to the bar was thrust open and Tex stormed in, shotgun raised, stock in his chest. He didn't allow for the step up and tripped and fell towards the chairs set to the left. His shotgun went off, scattering its load against the mirrors behind the optics. Glass shattered and fell like cascading sheets of ice; bottles were burst open and valuable whisky poured out. The angels had more than their share then.

Sat at the table to his right were Imogen and Jason, idly drinking from cans. Imogen put down hers, looked at Jason, then at the sprawled Tex and shouted over, 'Prick!'

Jason took one last pull of his warm drink and strode over to Tex. 'That could have been us, you dick.' He held out his hand.

Tex extended his, awaiting a helping hand up.

'Don't be even more of a dick than you need to be. Give me your weapon. Now.'

Tex's face reddened as he sheepishly handed it over.

Jason righted the table and placed the shotgun on it. 'You ever kill anyone?'

Tex sat up and shook his head.

'What happened at the farm? How did you get away?'

'I waited till they stopped roaming, got in my truck, then I met you both.'

'Get yourself gone. Make for the A90. Go south. I don't want to see you again. Take your shotgun. Don't aim it at us. Go now before she puts a bullet in you.'

Tex nodded slowly, his mouth open, ready to say something, but he saw Imogen raise her pistol. He rose swiftly, grabbing his shotgun, and ran out of the door.

Jason watched him go. He shook his head. 'Fucking liability.' He looked around at the devastation Tex had caused. 'Pippa and I loved coming here. The steaks were phenomenal.'

Imogen picked up a menu from the table where she was nursing a can of lemonade and idly scanned it, licking her lips as she read. A packet of salted peanuts was thrown down on the table.

'I need to pee. Enjoy these while I'm gone.' He strode off to the nearby gent's toilets, SA80 held at the ready as he went up the ramp of the corridor. Before he opened the door, he spied a camera above the frame. It had a red blinking light. He tried the light switch; it wouldn't illuminate anywhere.

Imogen opened the nuts and heard cubicle doors being kicked open, a shot echoing, as she held them up to her mouth and tipped back a mouthful. As she chewed, she emptied some into her palm and held them out for a grateful Sabre. She figured he'd need the extra salt, after all his exertions. Then, as they both continued to chew, she walked over to the bar, glass crunching beneath her boots, and took out a bottle of water. She found a deep plate and wedged both into her chest rig. Then she walked back to Sabre, lifting him up, letting out a groan at the weight of him, and walked outside, away from the broken shards of glass. 'Got to protect your paws, eh, lad?' She was rewarded with a rasping lick of her face and giggled at the sensation. She carefully put him down, then laid down the bowl and emptied the bottle into it. 'Here you go, boy. Now stay.' As she walked back to the building, she raised her middle finger in the air and shouted, 'You listening, fuckface? Some boots for Sabre's paws are needed when you resupply us.'

Sabre lapped up the water, not caring that some was trickling down his chin and more was spilling out onto the pavement, onto pretty, blue mosaic tiles. He then sat down, eyes upon the doorway. He didn't bother trying to make out what the shapes on the tiles were.

'One of my best men,' muttered the colonel to no one in particular. He paced the room, unsure of what to do. His creased face spoke volumes. Looking back at the screen seemed to make him more agitated, and he began fumbling at his notebook. 'Not that it matters. That mission is dead in the water, literally. But he should have got clear. Goddamned Russians.' He clenched and unclenched his hands, then strode to a nearby operator. Standing behind her, he grasped the back of her chair and peered into the monitor. 'It's no time to sit and have a drink.' Then he looked at the other side of the split screen. 'Even the dog is joining in. Tell gate eight to expect an arrival. Pity the fool lost his Stetson when we fired that missile. They could have used that as an indication of a friendly arriving.' Turning back, he added, 'Warn them to take the shotgun off the idiot first.' He began tapping a message on his mobile. He missed the raised finger playing out on the screen and the stifled laughter from the operator.

Jason shook himself dry at the urinal and began tidying away when he felt the buzz in his pocket. He heard the inevitable double alarm ping. Ignoring it, he went to wash his hands but stayed himself when he remembered the water would be off along with the power. Frowning as he exited, he wondered where Imogen was and headed out of the bar.

'I didn't want Sabre getting cut,' she explained, while scanning the area.

The dog looked up from his drink, dribbling water on Jason's boot.

Jason smiled. He knew she had a soft spot for the dog. He looked over to the sea and was rewarded with a red glowing sun, giving the last of its heat as it began its journey to dip below the horizon. 'It's getting dark, I hadn't realised. Let's find a room for the night. Best we stay together. We can lock the bar doors. I don't know if the infected have enough sense to unlock doors.'

'Maybe not room three. Your turn to carry the dog.'

'I'll leave him here. Let's clear the rest of the building first.'

They swiftly climbed the stairs again, checking in each of the rooms. They found the bar staff and what looked like the owner or manager of the restaurant and hotel. They had attacked each other, perhaps over working conditions. The Russians had struck in the morning, so the restaurant was empty. Jason and Imogen locked as many doors as they could, then went to their Land Rover, removed the kitbag with their cooker and rations and carried Sabre up to room six.

Once settled in the twin bedroom, Jason turned his attention back to the mobile phone. The instructions were simple: 'Kill all.' The colonel was a man of few words. Jason swallowed hard. He'd share this order with Imogen in the morning, after they'd fried their tins of bacon roll and spooned some of this Spam like meat into Sabre's bowl. He tapped his reply into the phone. 'Room 6. Switch on power and water. Need showers. It's been a long day.'

Within seconds the lightbulb above him sparked on and the dim bedside lights illuminated Imogen, getting to grips with the small gas cooker on the bedside table. She was looking forward to her mix in the bag ready meal. There was even a can of high-quality dog meat. She opened this first, tickled Sabre by the ear, and spooned the mixture onto the carpet. He wolfed it down, fluff and all.

'Window view bed, or nearest to the toilet?' asked Jason.

'You have the window one. I usually have to go in the middle of the night.'

'Pippa is the same several times a night. The baby presses down on her bladder.'

Imogen reached over and rubbed his arm, breaking his concentration at the memory.

He reached round and patted her hand. 'The shower is powered up with water and electric. You go first. Sabre's already had his bath. But let's eat first, I'm famished. It's tiring work, seeing you blow things up.'

'That was brilliant, wasn't it? I can't wait to try out these grenades.'

Jason sighed. He made a mental note to check the kitbags first during any future resupplies. He wondered if they'd find anyone alive tomorrow.

Chapter 8

Jason awoke to a furious scratching at the door. It took him a moment to rouse himself fully and realise where he was. It was the infected. He reached under his pillow for his Glock 19. That's when he heard the whimpering, like a little girl was in the room and crying for her mother. These were broken by deeper and louder grunts. A familiar voice shouted, 'I'm going to have you, Missy. Stop struggling. It'll be nicer for you and me.' Jason leapt out of bed and bounded over to the light switch.

The illumination revealed Tex atop Imogen. Her eyes were wide, like saucers. She was staring at the ceiling, like her mind was somewhere else, perhaps in her past. Her hands were pinned below the weight of Tex's belly. She tried to stop him from pulling down her knickers, but could only move her digits futilely. Tex turned around and winked at Jason. 'I'll have these off in a moment. Then we can take turns, me first.' He grunted as he tried to whip down the fabric and stopped when he felt the cold, hard plastic of

Jason's Glock 19 pressing down on his forehead. 'It's okay. Wait for your turn. No one will mind. There's no law. We won't get caught. We can do anything and get away with it.'

'That's right,' said Jason, as he pulled the trigger.

Sabre, in the corridor outside, scratched at the door some more. Splinters of wood were caught between his paw, where Tex had forced the lock with his crowbar and ushered the dog out with some rancid meat from the adjacent restaurant. Tex had then pulled a chair across the damaged door to stop the dog from returning.

The back of Tex's head erupted, spraying blood, bone, and grey brain across to Jason's bed. His head flopped forward, narrowly missing Imogen's skull. His sheer weight dropped, pinning her some more.

Jason holstered his weapon and then shoved Tex off his friend, letting the man's body roll onto the floor, into the gap between the beds.

Imogen scrambled back, head bouncing on the fabric of the headboard. She pulled her duvet up, covering herself up to the neck, drawing comfort from its high tog rating and bulk. She continued her whimpering.

Jason gently took her face in his hands and made soothing noises and after a few minutes, he drew her to him and held her tight. She was now making sounds which began with, 'S, s, s.'

It took him a few seconds to work out what she wanted, and he gently asked, 'You want Sabre?'

She tried to speak, but no further sounds came out, so she simply nodded furiously.'

Jason gently let her go and pulled the chair away from the door.

Black and brown fur rushed into the room; teeth bared. Sabre took one look at the still figure, cocked his leg, let go a foul stream of urine, then bounded up the bed and nuzzled ever so gently into Imogen.

She released her grip on the duvet and allowed it to fall. Jason looked away as it revealed her sports bra and midriff, but not before he saw her wrap her arms around the dog and hold him tight toward her as she began to sob.

The colonel strode into the Ops Room. 'Show me,' he snapped, not appreciating his sleep being disturbed. As he watched the clip, eyes feeling heavy, he became instantly awake as he watched the lock being forced. 'Well, well, well. That'll explain why he didn't turn up at the gate. What's he up to? Can you get me sound on this?'

The technician tensed her back. 'I'm afraid not, sir. The hotel system is one of the older ones.'

'Damn,' retorted the officer.

Jason thought about dragging the corpse out of the bedroom, but remembered the CCTV camera he'd seen in the corridor. He knew Army Intelligence would probably be hacked into it. He pulled on his combat clothing, boots, and chest rig, went outside, SA80 at the ready, and crunched through the glass, ensuring all the doors were locked again. He saw the point of entry through the gent's window. There was no way to fix it, so he strode off to the back room, delved deep into the trouser pocket of the manager's corpse and found a set of keys and returned and locked the toilet door. Then, after finding an undamaged glass and optic, returned upstairs, and sought another room, this time with a double bed and sofa.

'What are you up to, Flight Sergeant Harper?' whispered the colonel as the video operator clicked through a series of live feeds for the officer to watch. 'Are you recording this?'

'Yes, sir,' replied the corporal, glad of something to do, other than watching helplessly as people, or what were once people, tear each other apart.

Jason softly said, 'Let's move you to another room. I've a clean bed for you and Sabre.' He made a clucking noise and ushered them both to follow him.

Imogen rose, then saw the crowbar. She knelt to pick it up, then sprang onto the bed in one bound and leant over the body of Tex. She lifted her arms in the air and thrust the bar down through his face. An awful squelching sound came from the corpse as she dug deep, screaming as she used all her force to pin his face to the floor. Then she let go and uttered, 'You bastard. I knew you were creepy from the start. Rot in hell. No one does that to me. Not again. Not ever.'

A hand reached over to hers and gently took her hands, which were wrapped round tightly, off the crowbar. 'Come away, Imo. Let's get you somewhere safe.'

She allowed Jason to guide her off the bed and he removed one hand from her tight grip so that he could take out his pistol from its holster. Then he opened the door and led her to another bedroom while Sabre paced around them, not leaving Imogen's side for more than a few seconds. The trio made for a double bed, pushed farther into the corner of the well-decorated room. The bedding and cushions matched the other, without the blood splatters.

Jason laid her down gently, all the while talking softly to her, telling her she was safe. After the duvet was pulled over her, Jason patted the bed. 'Up, Sabre.'

The dog immediately sprang up to the bed and carefully padded up to Imogen, then nuzzled into her and was rewarded with a tight hug. Then the tears flowed.

Jason swallowed hard. He'd been fighting the rising bile at the sight of what the crowbar had done. He hadn't wanted to disappoint his friend in her hour of need by vomiting. Checking that the door was locked, he then dragged the two-seater sofa to barricade the entrance. It would be a tight fit for sleeping, but he'd manage. He'd slept in worse. He regretted not bringing their mats and sleeping bags. There was no way he was leaving her.

Imogen's sobs gave way to whimpering and soon she drifted off to sleep, arms tight around Sabre, whose eyes were still open and scanning the room. He, too, didn't want more harm befalling his tribe.

Jason bedded down on the sofa as best as he could, fully clothed, pistol in hand, SA80 rifle leaning against the fabric, chest rig tucked under his head as a makeshift pillow. He fell into a light sleep, like he had been trained to do in the RAF Regiment during exercises and deployment. He'd never fail her again.

Chapter 9

The aroma of sizzling sliced bacon roll filled the room, but the sound was drowned out by the hiss and splatter of the boiling water. Soon the bedroom smelled of ground coffee, in a bag, but a much-needed caffeine hit.

Jason awoke when he heard the water being poured from the pan above the camping gas cooker. He took a second to orientate himself, then tried to stretch out and bumped his limbs on the sides of the sofa. He uncoiled himself from the near foetal position and sat up, swinging his legs out, moving his rifle just in time to stop it from falling over.

'Morning Cowboy. No beans with your coffee. Porridge with apple flakes. Looks like sick, but is super tasty. Bacon roll for afters.'

Jason squinted at Imogen through his sleep deprived eyes, heavy with overnight grit. He rubbed them clean. 'You okay?'

Imogen tickled Sabre's ears as he tucked into another can of dog meat. This time it was poured into a small tray which used to hold the courtesy biscuits and mugs. The complimentary shortbread had been squirrelled away in a pouch in Imogen's tactical vest. She was wearing this chest rig over her combat uniform and looked the model fighting soldier. 'The fat fucker didn't hurt me. He couldn't get inside me. But he brought back some unhappy memories. They are back in their box now.'

Jason took that as a hint not to discuss it any further, so simply nodded and took the offered mug of coffee.

'I left the bag in. I know how much you like strong coffee. I didn't know you could get ground coffee in a bag. Clever that.' She stirred the bag of porridge and handed it to him. 'Careful. It's hot.' She looked him straight in the eye. 'Thank you.'

He rested his mug on the sofa arm and took the meal, swapping it between hands until it cooled. 'We're a team. I'm sorry I didn't waken sooner. I'm surprised I didn't hear the door being jemmied. I was so fatigued. It won't happen again.'

Imogen nodded approvingly at the sofa position. 'I mean, thank you for killing him. He wasn't infected.'

'In a way, he was. People like him disgust me. Like he said, there is no law now. Just us. He needed putting down. Taking him prisoner would have made him a liability. No one will ever know. We'll leave him where he is. I don't know what sort of clean-up operation will be run after we've moved out from Stonehaven, but it could be months before he's found. It'll be a puzzle amongst hundreds of thousands, all along our region. I doubt they'll investigate it, whoever they are.'

'It's one of the few things anyone has ever done for me. I know taking a life isn't easy for you.'

'It was in his case.' He sighed. 'Something similar happened to Pippa.'

'Oh?'

'She was on a girl's night out in Aberdeen. They'd booked a suite in one of the fancy hotels. They kipped in the same room, in the beds, sofas and chairs, when the nightclub kicked them out in the early hours. One of the single girls met a man and brought him back to the hotel lounge bar and ordered coffee. They stayed downstairs, chatting for another hour. Then he said goodnight to her and told her he'd just use the gents and book a taxi at reception. But he didn't. He waited for the receptionist to go into the back room for something, then slipped up the stairs. Pippa's friend hadn't locked the door, and he had weaselled the room number from her. She was well drunk and innocently gave it away. Anyway, he found the nearest woman in the dark and tried to rape her. He chose my Pippa.' Jason began clenching his fists. The pain from his nails digging into his palms made him stop.

'The bastard. Did he harm her?'

'No, she screamed the house down.'

Imogen looked to the floor. 'I just froze. Sorry.'

'Don't be. It's a natural flight or fight response. Psychological experts say there is now the freeze response. I'm sorry it happened to you, too.'

'Did the court's sentence him to much time?'

Jason laughed grimly. 'It didn't get that far. Her friends woke up, then beat the crap out of him! Some with slaps and fists, others used the heavy base of the table lamps. One even sprayed his eyes with perfume. His groin area took a lot of damage. There were no knives in the room, but they had some scissors in their makeup collection.' Jason winced at the thought. 'They told him the corridor CCTV would have captured him coming into the room and they were all witnesses to the attempted rape. During blows, they told him to shut his mouth and not do it again. Pippa tells me he was lucky to wriggle free and make his escape.'

'Did he go to the police?'

'No. I think he would have been too embarrassed to have it made public that he'd been beaten by a group of women. His dick would have needed medical attention, though. I wonder what he would have told the doctors and nurses at Aberdeen Royal Infirmary? I bet it made the Accident and Emergency teams' night.'

Imogen gave a brief smile. 'How did it affect Pippa?'

Jason took a sip of coffee and swirled it around his dry mouth. 'She began having nightmares and was edgy at bedtime. She was able to access free counselling through her work, all kept confidential. That helped, given time.' He grinned. 'Now we are expecting!'

'We'll get through that fucking fence and wipe the smirk from that colonel's face.'

'I know. And if you need to talk, I'm here.'

'Thank you. Now eat your breakfast. I want to kill me some zombies!'

Jason was about to correct her, to tell her they were people once. But he now knew that she knew this, deep down. He wouldn't correct her again. He tucked into his meal; it was the right temperature now.

Chapter 10

Imogen emptied the kitbag on the floor of the Land Rover, kicking aside layers of green pullovers, gloves, hats and waterproof jackets and trousers. She found what she needed nestled at the bottom. They were resting on top of some thermal tops.

'I'd be careful with those,' heeded Jason.

'Front towards enemy,' she read out aloud. 'My first claymore mine.'

He carefully pulled it from her in a quick game of pull, only he didn't want the surprise to go off. 'You want it under him, don't you?'

She nodded grimly. 'I don't want any evidence coming back to bite you later in life. You, Pippa, and your child deserve a peaceful life.' She looked around her. 'After all this is over.'

He shook his head. 'It was our favourite restaurant and pub.'

'It's for a noble cause.' She pointed to the nearby jetty. 'I'll park up there. I'll load up our rifles with fresh clips, then that'll be a good defence for when they come.'

He looked at the white-washed walls of the ancient building, then at the modern, glass-fronted restaurant, which afforded better views of the harbour, for the last time. 'Yes, that'll be far enough from any debris.'

'I reckon the explosion will have the zombies flocking this way. Then I can use The Long to pick them off and you can spot for me. I'll get my breathing in a good rhythm this time.' She pointed to the rectangular, arched dull green object. 'I guess it has a timer? You'll not be in any danger?'

'No, I'm quite adept at setting these.' He reached down and took a grenade from the box.

'What's that for?'

'Dental records. Don't ask.'

She couldn't help herself. 'You've done this before?'

He nodded grimly. 'We didn't want to leave evidence of a martyr. It was another time, another land. It's locked in my box. Along with twenty-two others.'

She understood. 'I'll leave you to it.'

They climbed off, Jason ran into the building as she and Sabre drove off. He didn't bother admiring it again. He'd said his goodbyes. He bounded back up to the room, took a deep breath and entered room six. The stench of dried blood engulfed his nostrils and took deep root in his senses. He fought the rising bile and as he stooped over what was left of Tex's face; he was thankful he'd died with his mouth open and didn't have to fight against rigor mortis. He tried to force the grenade carefully into the mouth. It wouldn't fit. Instead, he used his boots to roll the obese man over, tucking the corpse's hands under his immense girth as best he could, then turned his face slightly. The grenade was placed by his mouth, as if an apple within the jaws of a suckling pig roasted at a banquet. The claymore was wedged alongside the fingers so that no identifying digits remained when things went boom. Jason expertly set the timer, gave the corpse one last look, and muttered, 'See you in Hell, Tex, or whoever the fuck you were,' and ran from the room and building, not bothering to close any doors behind him. As he left the bar, he spotted one of the few malt whisky bottles to have survived Tex's ineptitude. He grinned when he saw it was a Glendronach Highland single malt.

The Land Rover had been expertly reversed along the single track of the sandy jetty. Imogen was settling the sniper rifle along the steel canopy of the roof. She laid out several full cartridge casings on what looked like a beanie hat. His spotter's scope was awaiting him.

He tipped the bottom up and down and the deep amber fluid sloshed in the three quarters full bottle. 'I found something to warm us up.'

'Cool. Sabre's had a drink. No ice-cubes or glasses?'

He looked aghast. 'What! Spoil a good dram. I don't mind slurping from the bottle if you don't.'

'Only with you, Cowboy. How long do we have?'

'Any moment no-'

An almighty explosion that seemed to rock their vehicle interrupted him and glass, wood, and bricks flew out of the hotel. The roof erupted like a volcano spilling its lava. Instead, traditional grey slate tiles and bits of timber spewed into the air, then came crashing down, taking bits of furniture, carpets, and curtains with it. There was no sign of the fancy bedding. Black plumes of smoke were sucked into the air and what was left of the buildings were ablaze. Jason now accepted his life would be totally different now, but for how long?

His thoughts were interrupted by the ringing of his phone. It could only be one person and he weighed up whether to answer it, but he did.

'What the fuck was that?' demanded the colonel.

'Er, an explosion, sir.'

'I can see that, you fuckwit. Why?'

Jason looked around him and saw the harbour CCTV cameras, probably to deter vandals. It hadn't worked. He looked back to the ruins of the hotel, bar, and restaurant and his handiwork. Being caught for vandalism was the least of his problems. The colonel was probably pissed that he'd lost his camera feed in the hotel. 'Got to go, they are here.' He slipped the phone away and took up his scope.

'Don't you dare hang up on me, you long streak of -' The colonel banged his fist on the nearest table, just missing the dainty hand of the camera operator.

She jumped at the unexpected noise and rush of air and cowered to her left, bumping shoulders with her colleague. She wished she hadn't been deployed here. Had it only been two days? It felt longer, trapped in this Portakabin, with all the testosterone exuding from every pore of the Mad Colonel, as he was already known when he wasn't in the room. She didn't know how much more she could endure of seeing victim after victim fall to the duo she'd been tasked to monitor and record. Her shoulders eased as she heard the officer storm away. The screen in front of her was now only split in two, accessing the harbour cameras located high on a lamppost. She didn't like what she saw, but kept to her duty, regardless.

'The smoke and fire may bring friendlies. Please check the eyes before firing,' pleaded Jason.

'Ready that, Flight Sergeant Harper? I'm all cocked and ready to fly.'

He grinned as he took a long pull from the whisky bottle and threw it behind him, where it landed on a green jumper with Velcro epaulettes and padded elbows. They'd issued them clothing from the Cold War era and he thought it apt. She'd refused a drink of the whisky and he mentally berated himself when he remembered her methadone. She's probably already taken a dose to help her forget last night and ease her through the day.

At the narrow junction to the harbour entrance a young man came running. He was bare chested and heavily tattooed. His belt buckle was loose and the leather beat against his groin with each step. It didn't seem to bother him as he stopped and appeared to sniff the air. Imogen shot him between his next breath and her holding her own. The bullet took him neatly through his nose and carved out a deep trench through his brain and exploded through the parting at the back of his scalp. Blood and gore splattered against the blackened walls of the building behind him, giving it an apt display of colour. It was an art gallery, specialising in selling oil paintings of the normally tranquil harbour and boats to tourists. The body crumpled.

A white handkerchief was thrust out of a row of dark painted sheds to the left of the Land Rover. Through his scope, Jason could see a shaking, wrinkled hand, then a man wearing a navy knitted jumper bobbed his head out. Jason put up his hand as if directing traffic and gave the stop sign. He shouted over, 'Stay back. Close the shed.' He counted along the row. 'Friendly in the fifth shed.'

'Copy that.'

He rolled his eyes and hoped she wasn't going all-American, like Tex, or Bob, or whoever he once was. He ran the scope along the row of sheds, large enough to store fishing nets, buoys, rope, and other equipment, rather than being used as beach huts. He wondered how long the poor man had been hiding in there and how he escaped the Russian jet fumes.

A large Stetson blew down the road and Imogen used this as a marker of the wind and adjusted the rifle. She didn't give Tex a second thought. She aimed down at the restaurant that was housed in a former fish factory or warehouse. It was on the top floor and diners had to climb steps to get to it, helping them work up an appetite for the delights within. Lobster was firmly out of her price range and she wondered if their little stove could cook one. There were bound to be several still alive in the massive tank. They probably had to show their customers how fresh their lunch would be. She made a mental note to go shopping. She read the museum sign and decided she'd not visit that building that occupied the ground floor. Museums bored her.

'I thought zombies were supposed to lose their flesh and have arms drop off after being infected,' puzzled Jason as he spotted a red-eyed man wandering out from the tourist information building to their right. 'He looks perfectly normal, like he's just asking for directions.'

'Clever fuckers, those Russians. I bet they want the infected to live as long as possible to kill off the troops and civilians, before they invade and take over our land, like they tried in Ukraine.'

Jason sighed; war bred clever weapons. He'd leave that one for the scientists. He watched as Imogen crouched by the side of the Land Rover, rested the rifle on top of the two kitbags she had dragged over, steadied her breathing, and shot the wandering man perfectly through one eye. A definite kill shot, just at the border range of the weapon. She was proving to be a better marksman, or rather markswoman, than he ever was.

The infected man fell against the glass pane of an artisan bread and cake shop. A streak of blood, like tomato ketchup, smeared the glass, as if trying to add flavour to the goodies on display. Jason spotted movement on the veranda above the shop, where coffees were enjoyed by customers. The view was normally delightful. He heard incoherent shouting and joined in. 'Stay where you are. It's not safe to come down. Don't go outside,' he warned.

Sabre growled to their immediate left and Jason turned and watched aghast as an infected woman was nearing the end of her climb up the ladder from one of the moored boats. 'You checked the boats?' he asked urgently.

'Whoops! Naughty me.'

Jason ordered Sabre, 'Kill, boy!'

The dog jumped from the vehicle and bounded over to the ladder, just as a hand stretched out on the top rung. A jaw clamped over the exposed wrist and dragged it on land. Her head bounced off the metal rung, where it curved into the harbour wall, and she lost consciousness. Her red eyes closed over as her body naturally tried to protect her eyes and her floppy head went thumping onto the concrete block, breaking her nose, forcing bone to meet brain, and killing her instantly. Sabre gave a few more tugs, then lost interest. He began sniffing along the jetty, pausing to look over the lip of the wall every few paces. He cocked his leg at one of the round metal tethering points and relieved himself. He was just finishing when he heard his mistresses whistle. He went bounding back onto the tailgate of the Land Rover.

Jason ordered him to stay while he jumped down, SA80 in hand. He ran along the jetty, looking at all the boats moored alongside. Their sharp whiteness and jolly painted motifs and names were lost to him. He was looking for the enemy. 'Stay put if you are uninfected,' he shouted out to those with closed cabins and deep hulls. 'Come out when the firing stops.' He didn't wait for or got a response. He ran back to the Land Rover in time to slot a red-eyed man crawling to the vehicle, out of sight from Imogen. There was a reason snipers needed a spotter and Jason proved how they keep their number ones safe. He jumped back on their firing point and picked up his scope. Imogen ignored him, steadied her breathing and he watched as The Long spat out another high calibre round. He heard a dull thud in the distance above the sound of the protesting gulls squawking overhead as another body dropped. He hadn't the opportunity to check its eyes.

Chapter 11

'I think we're done here.' He lowered his scope and watched as she shook her head vehemently.

'Can't you hear them?'

He strained, but all he could hear was the water lapping, the gulls, and the crackle of the fire as it found new fuel to burn through. Every so often a knot in a roof beam popped in the blaze, like a banger firework. He shook his head, but she didn't see his movement, as she was still looking down at her sights. The barrel of the weapon moved steadily from left to right and back again.

Then they broke through the smoke of the hotel just as some more roof and floor beams dropped and scattered a plume of ash into the air. A group of marching, almost stamping men, humming gently, but in some sort of rhythm, to their movements, came through the clouds of smoke, like soldiers crossing no-man's-land in World War One. Arms were down by their sides. This was no army movement, but a ragtag of civilian young men on the hunt for prey. They'd found it in them.

Imogen let off a steady flow of bullets that thinned their ranks as they ploughed their way through the rubble of the burning building and centred in on them. Several of the men fell over chunks of masonry, their heads taking the brunt of their falls. None of their arms were stretched out in a reflex motion to save their fall. They dropped like pins, skittles on a bowling alley. But they soon stood up and re-joined the march, ignorant of their pain and blood-flowing foreheads and scalps. The red liquid pooled around their eyes but did not blind them. It was as if they were centring in on the scent of Imogen and Jason alone as their nostrils twitched and flared.

Jason held his fire, knowing the SA80 bullets would fall short. He felt impotent against them and their sinister advance and willed Imogen to fire quicker. As the fourth body fell, she calmly changed her cartridge, the last full one on the beanie hat, and killed five more men in rapid firing. Their heads snapping back, almost like they were dance movements in a well-choreographed piece on a stage. Then she placed The Long down and unslung her SA80 and winked at him. 'Bet I can get more than you.'

He marvelled at how well she could switch her emotions from being sexually assaulted to being a killing machine. He knew this was not normal, but then their reality was no longer normal. He wondered what their mental health would be like after they'd completed this awful mission. If they survived. He shuddered.

Staying where they were, commanding the higher ground, they fired in unison, single bursts of well-aimed fire into the approaching crowd. Several more bodies fell, but still the crowd advanced relentlessly, like the aliens in the old Space Invaders game. All they needed was the nerve-jarring, pulse-quickening music.

From the corner of his eye, he saw her tilt her weapon and give it a shake. She'd got a stoppage and was frantically trying to clear it. He kept on firing and swiftly changed his magazine, like he'd been taught and drilled years ago. Unlike her, he wasn't counting.

He went from target to target and as the thinning crowd approached the entrance to the jetty; she threw down her rifle and calmly unbuttoned the side pocket of her combat trousers and from this thigh pouch took out her trusty black catapult and a box of large ball bearings. She placed the opened box on the roof of the vehicle and as quick as he could fire, she loaded and twanged back the catapult. He saw wide wounds open in flesh. Fresh blood was spilling onto the concrete. The tide held back, ready to wash it clean. One ball bearing smashed through askew spectacles but soon found a vulnerable eye to explode, its thick liquid running down a nose as another body fell.

A head of one infected man pulled back as a ball bearing entered his forehead, dead centre of his eyes. An involuntary surprised expression appeared on his face, as if he had been stung by a wasp. Only this one had a huge sting in its tail that burrowed deep into his brain, killing him instantly. He dropped to the floor, taking down the marching man behind him. They fell in an ungainly heap, and the unwounded man thrust his hands out to pull himself up. His thumb squelched into the dead man's eye socket, bursting through the sightless organ. He tugged it free and removed his moist digit.

Imogen twisted to her left, drawing a bead on a running man, trying to outflank them. Sabre was running towards him but not going as fast as the reloading of her catapult. A ball bearing whizzed through the air and penetrated his cheek as his head was turning to his left. It dug deep and exited through his other cheek, smashing teeth on its way. He didn't stop but simply spat the broken incisors and molars to the ground. Several flew onto Sabre's coat as he leapt at the man, the dog's intact, razor-sharp teeth clamping onto the severed cheeks, tearing, and pulling until the flesh came out in a huge chunk. Sabre chewed and swallowed, as fast as a hungry diner devouring a long-awaited meal, relishing this unexpected treat as the man fell over the dog's vast frame. Then Sabre began ripping and tearing at the exposed, mushy face, his tongue delving in deep, lapping up the fresh blood, exploring crevices and tasty pulp. He found the rich goodness of the tongue and tore it out with several pulls of his head, chewing, releasing an abundance of blood and tissue tastier than the treats his human companions had provided over the last two days.

Jason, seeing this from the corner of his eye, feeling bile rise at the sight, whistled for the dog. It came out at a low pitch as the sharp, acid reflux won and he vomited over the side of the vehicle, onto a short, infected woman who was trying to jump onto the side of the vehicle. Her weak arms floundering uselessly on the metalwork as she was scrambling ineffectually to get onboard. She was soon pulled down and trampled by taller infected who used her as a convenient springboard. Their heavy weight crushing her ribs as easily as a cardiac surgeon separating the sternum during a heart operation. The cracking echoed around the harbour. Her body went limp as her heart and lungs were pierced with broken bone.

Clawing hands reached the lip of the Land Rover's sides and were bitten back by Sabre, who, recalled from his tasty morsel, was now standing upon the killed woman. Several digits were shorn clean off by the dog's sharp teeth and fell amongst the empty shell casings.

Jason dropped his rifle, allowing the sling to save it from clattering to the floor. It bounced against his thigh and, ignoring the pain, he unholstered his Glock 19 and began shooting at the nearest men.

One looked like his favourite local singer, Colin Clyne, but he slotted him though his chest anyway as he was prising himself aboard. He fell with a heavy thud. He hoped the music industry would forgive him.

The inevitable click of an empty magazine surprised Jason, and before he could execute a rapid change, he felt a pair of hands at his throat tightening down. He fell against the cabin roof, then was pushed to his right, falling over the side, hands following him, locked tight. He landed on a pile of bodies, bloodying his clothing and knocking the wind from him. And still the hands clamped down. His breath-starved mind wondered why Imogen had stopped firing. Then he remembered his combat knife. He stopped trying to remove the hands and struggled to unsheathe it instead. Gratefully, he heard the metallic rasp as it unsheathed and then he stabbed and stabbed again, grunting, and shouting with each exertion. Hearing a repeated, 'Fuck you!' he didn't register for a few more stabs that it was him making the noise. The man fell on top of him, no longer gripping him. He went floppy and heavy. Jason lay for a few seconds, getting valuable air to his lungs, then he heaved him off. Staring and laughing from the back of the Land Rover was Imogen.

'What the fuck!' he blurted out. 'You could have helped me.'

'What? And spoil all your fun.'

Jumping to his feet, he looked around. Piles of bodies, again. Another killing field and only a small part of the town. He bent down to the corpse and pulled out his knife, not relishing the squelching sound. He tried wiping it clean on the nearest body and sheathed it, not caring that blood still dripped from it. He laughed, despite the gruesome situation. His Imogen was back in fine form.

A black and red packet with Thistles and a Castle pictured on the wrapping was thrown his way and he expertly caught it in a reflex movement.

'Enjoy some shortbread, Cowboy, we're supposed to be on holiday.'

The camera operator let off a deep sigh as her tense shoulders drooped. She'd been holding her breath during the struggle, silently rooting for the Flight Sergeant, watching in horror as his companion, the feral women as she nicknamed her in her head, stood and watched after felling the last of the mob with what looked like a toy straight from the Oor Wullie cartoon strip in the annuals her younger brother got each Christmas from their Scottish granny. She was glad her favourite relative lived in Auchtermuchty, many miles away from this battlefield. The yellow chemicals from the Russian jet had not penetrated that far south. She wished she was there now, having the comfort of being looked after by the older woman, tasting her homemade tattie scones, hot from the griddle pan, lathered in salted butter and washed down with tea so strong you could paint a shed with it.

The operators to her left and right had even joined in the viewing while keeping an eye out for the return of the colonel. Their screens in their locations had shown no movement for several hours. They were leaning over like two stretching giraffes surrounding her. She knew Phillip, the sergeant to her left, kept a kill count for their mobile canteen wall. Their officer never entered there. It was too beneath him. A grisly tally that she took no pleasure from. The feral woman was leading.

Chapter 12

Jason's hand, shaking, blood encrusted, pointed to the shed. He took another swig of water from the bottle and then splashed some on his hands and tried to wash away the evidence of his crimes. It had little effect. He leaned over, readying himself for the inevitable vomiting. It didn't come. He chanced a piece of biscuit from the hotel room, using the clean wrapping to unfurl the treat so that no blood contaminated it. He felt like a theatre nurse unpacking her equipment before a long operation. The sweet crunch and instant sugar rush acted as a balm that calmed his racing heart. He chewed one shortbread finger before giving in to Sabre's sad puppy eyes and gave him the other.

Looking around the devastation, he suddenly remembered, 'The old bloke in the shed.'

Imogen bundled her catapult back into her trouser pocket. 'I hope he had a potty in there. I bet he shat himself!'

Jason sat himself on the lowered tailgate, catching his breath. He reached over for the whisky bottle and took a long gulp. It burned on the way down and dampened his bile. 'In that case, I'll let you go over and rescue him. I'll check the boats. I'm sure someone is in the locked cabin in the third one.' He walked away before she could argue.

She turned to Sabre, 'It can't stink more than the mighty poos you curl out.'

Sabre nudged his muzzle into her hand and followed her, taking the time to sniff at the fresh corpses and lick some blood from the nearest.

'You can come out now. It's safe. I promise,' Jason gently declared. He'd climbed down the mooring ladder after first kicking a body into the water.

Movement could be heard, and the boat gently swayed with the tide. 'Who are you?'

Jason summed up the question for a few seconds and then replied, 'The military. No infected people are in the area. I have a rifle and will protect you.'

The door opened a fraction. 'Show me your eyes.'

Jason tried to smile to show he was friendly and peered through the gap at a Japanese-looking woman in her thirties. A girl, about ten, was cowering behind her. Both were wearing facemasks.

'I'm clean. The chemical attack by the Russians is over. We are here to take you to safety.'

'We were wandering around town. Then people started attacking each other. We ran back to our boat. But each time we tried to unmoor her; we would get attacked. We stayed in the cabin. We've a toilet and a well-stocked galley and bedrooms. We were travelling the world together. After I lost my husband.' Tears welled in her eyes and her child reached round and took her hand.

'You are safe now,' repeated Jason. 'The military are stopping boats from leaving the area to prevent the infected from spreading.' He didn't have the heart to say they would have been gunned out of the water by the helicopters that were patrolling the coast. They had been lucky not to have sailed off. 'Come on out.'

The door opened fully, but the couple kept their masks on. 'You can take any belongings you can carry. I can't help. I must be ready to fire my rifle.'

'Thank you, we'll quickly pack a bag.'

'I'll keep watch from atop the ladder. Be as quick as you can.'

'Hey, wrinkly, you can come out now.'

'Learn some fucking respect,' said a croaking voice as the shed door was opened. A craggy, bearded face looked around him while Imogen glanced in to see if there was anything useful to take.

'Right you are, granddad. Fought in the war, did you?'

'I'm not that old, you cheeky cow,' came the retort.

Imogen smiled. She took an instant liking to the feisty old man. 'How did you survive the chemical attack?'

'Is that what it was? The town's gone crazy.' He coughed and spat out some heavily stained sputum to the side of him, away from her. 'That'll explain why I survived. I was painting my shed. I wore a mask to protect my lungs from the paint fumes. I have pulmonary disease, so must be careful. It takes forever, but it is something to do. I can't go to sea these days and don't want my shed taken off me by the harbour committee. Me and a few old skippers come here to have a coffee and talk about the old days. We like to watch the new skippers unload their catches.' He looked around the harbour, eyes growing wider as he scanned the devastation. 'That was our local.' He shook his head.

'Follow me,' commanded Imogen as she turned away from the room with its assorted battered armchairs, table, kettle, and mugs. A few coils of rope and netting hung on the walls as decoration rather than useful equipment.

Sabre gave the man's outstretched hand a sniff and turned to follow his mistress.

The man gave his shed a last, fond look, shut the door carefully, took out a key and locked up his treasures. He shuffled after the woman, lagging as he carefully stepped over brick, glass, and pieces of wood, some still smouldering. He watched as she joined another man, dressed in similar camouflage gear, shouldering the same looking rifle. They were joined by two nervous looking women, one much smaller than the other, both cuddling close to each other, as if seeking comfort from each other. He didn't blame them; he too was terrified. He drew near and looked around him, expecting more military. He frowned when he saw no more.

Jason walked ahead. 'Follow us. I think he's blocked the way.'

The two women and the man's eyes squinted at the soldier, but soon fell in step. Imogen took up the rear and smiled at Sabre as he darted around the small column, making sure her charges were safe. The dog stopped to pick up a hand, blown clean off in the explosion. It looked feminine and young, like it had belonged to one of the dead restaurant servers. 'Leave,' she ordered.

Sabre let off a small whine of disappointment as he dropped the hand. The fingers wobbled on the road momentarily, as if trying to walk to the pavement, then laid still.

Banging on the window reminded the pair that there were customers in the cake and coffee shop. Imogen waved for the pair of twenty-year-old men, dressed in smart, but crumpled suits, to come out. Neither wore ties and their shirts were opened, revealing their slim necks.

The door cracked open, and a head popped out and looked around, then both men slowly came out of the shop and began running towards them.

Movement from the adjacent alleyway caught Jason's eye, and he watched in horror as two women, one bare chested, with large breasts wobbling like family-sized jelly, sprinted after them. Both had blood around their mouths. They knocked into the men, forcing the surprised pair to the ground, and began feeding on them. The male screams were curtailed as each of their oesophagus was torn open, almost simultaneously in the frenzied feeding. Jason instantly aimed his rifle, but his instincts were a fraction too late. He shot both women, and they fell on their victims. All four were dead. 'Look away,' he commanded of the young woman and her daughter.

The town was eerily quiet, save for the crackling of the fire. This receded as they rounded the corner. Even the gulls seemed to take the morning off. No doubt they'd be flocking to the former hotel and restaurant where goodies laid on the road for them.

Jason broke the silence. 'Thought so. The stupid fuc-' He stayed his tongue as he remembered the child. His face reddened, and he strode off to the Toyota pickup truck, which was wedged between a mobile home and a lamppost. He rummaged in his pocket and took out a key. He'd taken this from Tex's pockets, along with any other identifying items like his wallet. That was now at the bottom of the North Sea. Thrown out as far as possible when he was waiting for mother and daughter to pack several bags. Jason pointed to the back of the truck. 'Toss your bags in there.' He glanced at the woman's short legs and then turned to the old man. He was taller and could reach the pedals. 'Can you drive this?'

'I'd be happy to. This belonged to that idiot Bob. Is he dead?'

'Yeah, Bob didn't make it.' Jason watched as a flock of gulls swooped overhead. His remains will soon be long gone too, he thought.

'Small mercy. He bored us all with his tall tales. He soon emptied a bar when he walked in, looking for company.'

'Slam her in reverse and you'll soon get her out of there. Don't worry about scratching the motorhome. I guess we are long past caring about things like that. Go south. You'll find a fence at the county border. Stop there.'

The old man sucked in a breath. 'You've built a fence? Over the road? Already?'

'Yes, a fence has been built. To contain the infected. You'll get processed there.'

The old man looked back towards the harbour area. 'I've worked here all my life. I've never seen the like.'

Jason whirled around as a wheely bin began shaking. The lid flew off and a young man sprang up, like a jack-in-the-box. As Jason neared him, weapon at the ready, he wrinkled his nose at the smell of bin juice. He lowered his weapon as he saw the man raise both arms in the surrender gesture.

The young man then shrugged his shoulders. 'It was the only safe place I could think about.' He pointed to a biker's helmet. Inside was a snood with skulls adorning the black fabric. 'I was delivering pizza. Just my luck to dive into a bin with a pepperoni pizza. I hate pepperoni. I'm starving now.'

Jason laughed as he bid the young man to, 'Climb aboard. Best you take the back of the truck and hang on, you stink mate.'

'This situation stinks too. I don't know what's happening. Just get me out of here.' He jumped up on the back of the truck, his wet trainers leaving a trail of slimy bin juice after him.

'Don't stop for anything,' warned Jason to the old man. 'Not even if the lad in the back starts screaming. Drive fast and this'll plough through anything, or anyone.'

The old man gulped as he inserted the key in the ignition. A bloodied piece of paper was given to him. It was torn from a restaurant order pad.

Jason stowed away his pen and notepad, taken from the pocket of one of the dead waiting staff. 'If you get a chance to go to that address, or phone the number when you find a working telephone, tell her I'm safe, and I'll be home one day.'

The man's brow furrowed. 'Okay. Aren't you allowed to call home?'

'It's a long story.' He bobbed his head into the cabin and saw that the mother and daughter were settled. 'Buckle up.' He stepped back and watched as the old man gunned the accelerator and with a screech of protesting metal, the pickup carved a gouge out of the motorhome and reversed, did a three-point turn and gunned out of the street. No one waved goodbye. Certainly not the young man. He was hanging on for dear life.

'Well done, Cowboy. Now let's clear up the rest of this here old town!' quipped Imogen as she slotted a fresh magazine into her SA80 rifle.

Chapter 13

The telephone shrilled. 'Fuck off,' muttered Jason as he obediently pulled it out of his pocket. He hit the green button and drawled, 'Hello,' left a gap, then, 'sir.'

'Less of the shit. You'll treat me with respect and don't you ever hang up on me again, understood?'

'Of course,' a gap again, but slightly longer this time, 'sir.'

'We've detected heat signatures coming from the block of flats you're standing in front of. Second floor. The flat is to the left as you face the building. They are in the rear room. Three close together. We think they are friendlies. Bring them to me.' The line went dead.

Jason ran to the other side of the road and tried to peer in to the flat, but every curtain was pulled close. They'd have to do this the hard way. 'We'll have to check out the second floor. It'll mean clearing each flight of stairs together.'

Imogen stared up. She counted ground, first and then second. 'Why's it always the top floor?' she muttered as she cocked her rifle, ran to the block of flats, and booted open the door. Sabre close by her heels.

Jason shook his head. 'So much for stealth.' He ran after her, rifle at the ready.

The two ground-floor flat doors were shut, no signs of struggle, scratches or blood were on the doors, the welcome mats, or the well-attended flooring. Their filthy boots were about to upset a house-proud tenant. He aimed his rifle up the stairwell as she mounted the steps, crouched, waved him on, and aimed hers up the next flight of stairs.

An ajar door bothered Jason, and he hissed, 'We'd better check in here, cover me.' He pushed the door wider with his rifle muzzle. The smell assailed him and he gulped a few times. He entered a large hallway, jackets hung neatly in a row. They were all sizes, from toddler through to adult. Lying in the bathroom to his left was a small boy. He was on his back and a pool of blood had dried around him, as if trying to draw an outline around his prone figure. Jason didn't bother checking for a pulse. Instead, he pulled the shower curtain aside and checked the bath was empty. It wasn't. An older child, a girl, probably no more than seven, stared back at him with unseeing eyes. He reached over, closed her eyes, took a few steps to the toilet, lifted the lid, and vomited. He didn't bother trying to flush. Wiping his face on tissue paper, he allowed it to drop to the floor. He closed the eyes of the boy on his way out. Then he opened the nearest bedroom and was relieved to find it empty. So was the next one. The narrow kitchen straight ahead was empty too, with nowhere to hide. Jason walked to the lounge door, not caring that his boots echoed along the narrow corridor's wooden floor. He wanted someone to come rushing out so he could expunge his anger by spray shooting them on automatic. He was disappointed. The mother or father, or both, who had killed the children, had fled the flat, probably to feed on others. Jason doubted Social Services would be informed of their negligent actions. He punched the door, his combat gloves absorbing most of the pain. He wrestled it free from the cheap plywood, not caring about the damage he was causing to this Aberdeenshire Council owned building. He knew he'd never be sent a bill. He walked out, but hesitated in the bathroom. It seemed wrong to leave the two children there. 'Sorry,' he impotently whispered to them, then turned and left. He croaked out a 'Clear' warning to Imogen. Then coughed and found his voice. 'I'll enter the flat with the three heat signatures. I know the layout.'

Imogen had no time to argue as he mounted the stairs. She joined him in a small corridor as there was no other stairwell going up. Just the ceiling with a loft access panel which was securely bolted.

Jason booted open the door, then went storming from room to room. He found them in the kitchen. They were feeding from a tray of raw, rancid mince. Some fell from their mouths like live worms as they jostled for the meat. Their faces and necks had dried blood down them and their eyes were as red as the meat they were devouring like locusts once were. Jason flicked his safety catch to automatic and watched as they shuddered and danced as he fed his bullets into their undead bodies, bringing their suffering to an end and expunging his anger. He wondered which of the three were the parents and how he could play a family man after this mission was over. Tears ran down his cheeks as his bullets dried up and the dead man's click echoed around the cramped kitchen. He fell to his knees in despair, allowing his rifle to thud onto the linoleum.

Imogen came rushing in to find him curled up in a ball, hugging his knees, crying. She knelt by him and cradled him, their chest rigs doing the embracing as they bumped awkwardly. 'They are in a better place now.' She looked at the carved-up trio bleeding out by the fridge. 'But it's not them you are crying for?'

He uncurled himself, sat against the cooker, and shook his head, sending snot in the air.

Imogen spotted some kitchen towel, rolled out a few sheets, and handed them to him.

Jason dried his tears and blew his nose. He let the kitchen towel fall to the floor, then stood up. 'There were dead children in the flat below. The first I've seen close. On this mission, anyway.'

She nodded her understanding. He had a lot packed away in that box in his head. Some memories must have lifted the lid off and leaked out. Holding out her hand, she led him into the lounge and sat him on the sofa. She left him to compose himself while she shut the flat door, to stop the undead wandering in unannounced. She quickly checked the rest of the flat, then returned to the kitchen and found a clean glass from a cupboard and returned to him, putting the glass in his hand. From the table, she picked up an opened vodka bottle and poured him a small amount. When he lifted it to his lips, she saw his shaking hand. Some liquid dropped from the tumbler as he raised it to his lips and swallowed it whole.

Imogen walked to the window and feigned looking out so that he would think she hadn't seen his trembling hand.

The phone shrilled, breaking into their lapsed silence. Imogen returned to him and took it from his pocket. 'What?'

'What, sir?' came the indignant retort.

'Fuck off. The three are now dead. They were zombies.'

'Zombies? I wish our scientists knew what to call them. Zombies are supposed to rise from their graves, not be immediately turned while breathing in chemicals. I'm sure our boffins will come up with a suitable name soon.'

'Your scientists can fuck off, too. They should have found a cure. Open your gates, we want through. We are done here.'

'You can get to fuck now,' came the relished reply. 'Your mission is far from over.'

'I'm not in the military.'

'You are now. This is government sanctioned killing, remember. Now get moving. We've picked up over a dozen heat signatures to your north, and they are moving towards you.'

She hung up.

'What the fuck!' blurted the colonel. He hadn't finished with his orders. 'Fucking civilians!' he roared.

Backs remained ramrod straight as video operators stared intently at their screens, trying not to cheer for Imogen.

The operator who had hacked into the flat's internal CCTV, probably installed by a controlling boyfriend, watched with her heart being tugged as the women led Flight Sergeant Harper gently to his feet. He was already combat weary.

'You good? You got this?'

He slotted in a fresh magazine and wiped imaginary vomit from his lips. 'Let's do this.' Jason strode off to the door, rifle tucked into his shoulder, eyes looking down at his sights.

Imogen looked at Sabre, 'That's our boy!' Grinning, she clucked at the dog to follow. Before stepping out of the flat, she glanced at the hanging jackets and noted the bulge in the women's one and quickly rifled through the pocket, pulled out a purse, pocketed the banknotes and allowed the rest of the contents to fall on the floor.

Chapter 14

'Shall we go on foot for a while? I need the fresh air. If we're going to be attacked, I'd rather have access all around us. Let's find them and take the attack to the enemy. I've had enough of being defensive. Let's clear this town and get back to the fence.' Jason raised his rifle and looked down the row of flats. 'Colonel, if you are listening, and I know you are, I'd like a means to know when the enemy is coming so we can get into a firing position. Bring us something on the next supply drop.'

Imogen couldn't help but look up in the sky. She wondered if the drone that was tracking her looked like the ones she'd seen Mountain Rescue use in the hills to trace lost hillwalkers. She'd seen a television programme about it once, in prison. She gave up and followed Jason. He was walking in a semi-crouch, weapon raised and walking past a puppet shop. She looked in the window at the brightly painted costumes the comical-looking marionettes were wearing. 'The fuck you looking at,' she sneered at one. 'Who even buys this stuff?' Then she saw the crocodile with the exaggerated teeth. 'Mind you, I might come back for you later.'

'They are approaching, near to the bridge. They aren't quite in range. Let them get to the middle of the bridge. We'll set up over that car boot. Pity we don't have The Long.'

She fingered her grenade, buckled onto her chest rig, ready to pull out and throw.

A car had smashed through a fish and chip takeaway and was rammed home near the high counter. The blue framework of the shop was hanging down, the glass smashed through. She pointed to the other side of the pavement for Sabre and he dutifully strode over, sniffing at the nearest lamppost. She nodded at the glass and looked up at the sky. 'Definitely get some of those special dog boots. There is glass everywhere.' She was resigned to never getting through the fence. She knew the colonel would send them to another town or village each time they cleared one. She hadn't the heart to tell Jason that, though.

'Oh, man,' she shouted over to him. 'I loved a fish supper from here.'

He grimaced. 'As did I. The second-best chipper in Aberdeenshire. Home to the deep-fried Mars Bar.'

'Yuck! Even I have standards. Where's the first best chipper?'

He laughed as he crouched by the back tyre and pointed to the boot. 'Figured you'd need a rest over the boot. There's only room for one and you need to get over your loss!'

'Maybe that prick of a colonel can arrange for a chopper to emergency drop us hot fish and chips. A hunky paratrooper can abseil down and hand two over. With a pickled egg and onion chaser.'

'Paras are supposed to parachute in.'

'All right, Flight Sergeant Harper, all this military lark is new to me.' She took her left hand from her rifle and threw up a mock salute.

He rolled his eyes. 'That's wrong on so many levels.'

She looked down the road as a man and woman, sniffing the air as they went, noses high, like two prudes walking through a council estate, crossed the bridge. 'Close enough?'

'They are all yours.'

She shot them both in quick succession, through their foreheads. Their heads snapped back, unbalancing them as they fell, dangling them over the brickwork of the wall. They fell into the river. 'That's going to upset the view.' She remembered how pretty this river was, as it meandered down to the sea. And like these corpses, she used to tip her rubbish into its steady flow. She didn't like to say aloud that it would have been discarded purses and wallets, after she'd taken out credit cards and cash. She wondered if one might have been his.

Another of the undead came shuffling down from the bridge, his left arm hanging low. It had been dislocated at the shoulder, but wasn't appearing to cause him any pain. Jason put him out of his misery and cursed as his shot missed his intended forehead and smashed through its top teeth, obliterating years of dental care in an instance. His bullet still found the brain as it ploughed its way through and ended the man's misery.

More were running down the street now, passing rows of shops. Not giving them a moment's glance. They had smelled fresh blood and were seeking it out, like a dog to a rabbit's scent. Sabre began growling, teeth bared ahead, waiting for his attack command.

'Stay Sabre,' ordered Jason, not wanting the dog to take a stray bullet. He glanced behind him. No enemy was approaching. He beaded his rifle sight. 'I'll take the one on the left.'

Sensing a quick kill competition, Imogen shot at the one on the right. Her bullet went wide, narrowly missing the man's ear. It ploughed through and found a victim a few metres behind, puncturing a hole through his shoulder and clean through. It didn't put him down nor slow his striding. She wriggled further across the boot and adjusted her aim and found her mark. But not before Jason had shot and dropped his target. Seconds later, hers was down on the pavement, decorating the paving slabs a deep red.

Four men appeared in the road, coming from one of the side streets. Each was dressed in high-vis vests and the same boots and black clothing, with padding around their knees. They looked like builders and had the muscular frame that goes with the job. Imogen flicked to automatic and stopped them in their tracks, their bodies dropping in a mess of limbs.

More followed them, streaming out of buildings and down the same side street. These were running, teeth snarling, dried blood caked their molars, chins, and necks. Jason began calmly picking them off one by one, trying to ignore the rising tension caused by Sabre's insistent barking.

They were closing in. Only ten metres away. Imogen lost vital seconds changing her magazine and was regretting the indulgence of automatic fire. As she slotted in another magazine, she heard the regular ping of fire coming from Jason's weapon. She envied him his years of weapons drill. There was only so much you could learn from Call of Duty. She flicked back to single shot and began choosing the nearest undead.

One sprinted to his left, going around the pile of corpses littering the pavement and overspilling onto the road. His hands were outstretched, ready to grab.

The duo, concentrating on the crowd, missed him in their blind spot, and Sabre's high-pitched barking and snarling was just background noise now.

The running man hit the car bonnet from the side, almost knocking over Jason. He found his victim and wrapped his hands around Imogen's throat and began tightening his grip. They fell backwards in a writhing heap.

Jason saw this from the corner of his eye but was also alarmed at how close the eight deep undead were. He stopped firing, stood up, pulled off a grenade from his chest rig. The firing pin remained in place on his combat vest, arming the explosive. He expertly threw it, not shouting out a warning to Imogen. She was far too busy to care. Instead, he yelled, 'Sabre, defend,' and pointed to Imogen.

Sabre immediately sprang, his desire to protect his mistress was now realised. In three bounds, he crossed the road and sank his teeth into the undead's left ankle, finding flesh just above the low boot. He began pulling backwards, like he was wrestling a soft toy with his owner.

The undead kept his grip on Imogen, not feeling the death-like clamping down of the dog's teeth as blood poured from his leg. He slid down a few inches, affording room for Imogen to slide out her combat knife. Despite her lack of breath and purple pallor, she turned her shocked features into one of relish and was slicing through its throat as Jason's grenade went off. She spat out as she tried to suck in air as the fingers released their death grip. They were showered with flesh, bone, and rubble, as if a butcher had pelted them with offal while his construction pal used building debris.

Jason looked down the empty street, then brushed human remains out of his hair. 'Two helmets, bring us them on our next supply drop. You hadn't thought of everything.' He appeared to be shouting at thin air, his eardrums still stunned from the nearby blast. He looked across the once picturesque eighteenth-century bridge. The road was still passable, but the pavement and walls were in ruins. The council would need a larger budget from the Scottish Government this year, if it wasn't to put up its monthly council tax to any surviving citizens. He felt they were a two-person wrecking team.

Imogen sprang to her feet, looking for fresh targets, fingering her grenade, itching to use it, 'Son of a bitch,' she muttered as she marvelled at the severed head that rolled across the road and came to a rest at her feet. Its bared teeth looked like it was laughing at her. She booted it away, jealous that Jason got to use their new toy first.

Chapter 15

Jason leaned over what remained of the bridge wall, eyes closed. He was drawing in deep breaths to dampen the rising bile. After a few seconds of listening to the relaxing sound of the steady stream of water from the narrow river below him, he opened his eyes and wished he hadn't. A child, a boy, face frozen in fear, gently made its way down with the water, as if learning to float in the long defunct swimming pool at Bon Accord Baths in Aberdeen. An adult soon joined him and they cracked heads, a sound that grated on Jason's teeth. He brought his hand to his mouth and swallowed hard. Both had their chests and abdomens ripped open and appeared to have been eviscerated. The river had sluiced their empty cavities. Jason succumbed to the struggle and let out a torrent of vomit. He was wiping at his mouth when he felt a hand on his shoulder.

Imogen leaned over, 'Fuck me, that must have hurt the poor sods. Best not to look, Cowboy.'

'It's a bit late. It's all a bit too late. The sights we've seen. The things we've done. Oh, my God.'

'I know, right?' She watched him turn to her, and she saw his crunched-up face. Tears were welling in his eyes. 'Sorry. Not the time. This mission, if you want to call it that. Neither of us asked for it, but we are here and must play the cards we are dealt.' She pointed all around her. 'They weren't human. They wanted to kill us. They'd have ripped our throats open, and we'd be like those poor sods in the river.' Then she pointed to the boy and man, just before they continued their journey under the bridge. She repeated herself, emphasising each word. 'That could be us one day. We must keep going. It's them or us.'

'I know, it's just so needless, all the killing. It's ghastly.'

She reached into her chest rig and pulled out a protein bar and handed it to him. 'Compliments of the ration packs in the Land Rover. Eat it, you'll feel better. All this vomiting and retching, you need to get it under control. You're losing valuable nutrients. You are no good to me if you are feeling weak. Now start munching.'

He tore off the wrapper and bit down. As he chewed, he pointed to her bulging pouch, swallowed, then asked casually, 'How's the stash coming along?'

Her face reddened. 'Er.'

He laughed. 'Don't worry. No law, remember. I'm back in the military, so I will be getting my daily pay again. Hell, my pension pot is probably building up again. And it is index linked. I doubt the colonel will be paying you.'

'It's a shame to waste all that cash.'

'And rings.'

'You've seen me?'

'Yeah. The medical services had a nickname for the army medics: the Royal Army Medical Corps, the RAMC, was Rob All My Comrades. It goes back to the First World War, I think. There was a fallacy that stretcher bearers would strip bodies, or those dying or unconscious, of their watches and rings. I doubt it happened. They were too busy saving lives and dodging bullets and bombs. Brave men.'

'And so are we, in a way. We are putting them out of their misery and trying to save the uninfected.'

Jason pondered this for a moment. 'And following orders. That was the SS and Nazi excuses. What if we get through this, through the fence, what then? Will we be tried for crimes against humanity?'

She didn't like to tell him they may not survive. 'I hope the Russians get tried. It's their fault all this is happening to our region, and possibly further. We just don't know.' She ruffled Sabre's ears as he trotted up to her. 'Be like a dog, live in the moment.'

He turned away from the river and sat on the wall, juggling between the debris. 'I have my orders, but worry about you.'

'Don't. I'm a born survivor. Shall we get back to the Land Rover or continue on foot?'

He checked his ammunition pouch and instantly regretted the indulgence of automatic firing. 'I'm down to my last clip. The colonel hasn't phoned in new orders. Shall we go on foot to the Market Square and have a mooch around? We need to find somewhere safe for tonight. Then we'd better try to find survivors. They might be hiding from us. Our weapon sounds may have frightened them.'

'Let's hope dipshit's thermal imagining can see through floors and walls. I'd be hiding in cellars if I had the choice.'

He was about to say, not creepy Tex's though, but thought better. Best keep that box shut for the meantime. 'Let's walk.'

They stayed silent as they sauntered up the middle of the road. Cars had been abandoned across the pavements. Shop doors were left ajar, and they didn't bother checking any of the bodies. They were already bloating and changing to a purple colour. Imogen didn't have the heart to remove jewellery as she went. Instead, she kept her rifle raised, ready for the next attack as they passed a betting shop.

Jason stopped outside a pub. The door was shut, and he was staring at the window. A poster announcing an American tour of local singer Colin Clyne proudly boasted the states he'd be in, along with dates. Yesterday's date was bang in the middle of his Louisiana visit. He had escaped the chemical attack. Jason hoped his family was with him.

'I need to use a toilet,' declared Imogen as she looked around her. 'A proper one. It's all right for you, peeing wherever you like.'

Jason tried the pub door. It was locked. He raised his leg, then booted it open. The old lock easily gave way. He went in first, rifle at the ready.

They were sprawled over the beer pumps. Something had been eating away at the bar staff's faces. Jason leaned over the counter and picked up two tea towels from the drip tray area and covered what was left of their heads. Then he jumped over, opened the fridge, and took out two warm bottles of Cola. He grabbed a bottle opener as he squeezed past the bar staff. He sat down, exhausted. He didn't even have the energy to point out the ladies' toilet to Imogen as she unslung her SA80 and rested it on the bar. He slid a bottle across the table and then drunk deeply from his.

'Fucked if I'm using the bar toilet. They are always filthy and stinky. I'll go upstairs.' She pulled out her

Glock 19, leapt over the bar, peeked under the towels, tore down a strip of pork scratchings from the wall, and disappeared through the doorway, with Sabre in hot pursuit.

The colonel glanced around the monitors. Each screen had detailed road maps, showing streets and lanes. Dots were moving on all, bar one. He scanned the screens as he walked to his regular spot. Teams of two, sometimes four, or a three, were moving steadily along the other screens. He rested behind the young operator, her eyes willing something to happen on her screen. 'Why have they stopped? What's happening? Can you patch me into a live feed? Now!' he demanded with a quiver in his voice. His left eye began twitching. He scratched at it, his hand moving as fast as the tics.

The operator swiftly moved her mouse and typed on her keyboard. A grainy image of a long bar with old-fashioned benches around the edges appeared on the screen. Slumped back on the upholstery was Flight Sergeant Harper, head facing dejectedly down.

He had an empty bottle in his hand, his weapon on the table in front of him. His eyes were staring at the varnished floorboards.

'It's no time for a fucking NAAFI break.' The colonel reached for his phone and dialled. The tone rang out after a few minutes.

A packet of Mr Porky scratchings boasting a smiling butcher in a boater straw hat and white apron was thrown across the table and came to a halt on the edge. Jason looked up at it but did not return the smile. Instead, he stared at Imogen. 'The fuck are you wearing?' A grin cracked his solemn features, and the sparkle returned to his eyes.

Imogen reached behind her and pulled out two poles. A harness had been secured under her chest rig. Metal slid from two sheaths that ran down her shoulders and back, and she half-squatted as she drew out two martial arts swords and began waving them about and making grunting and high-pitched screaming noises. Then she stopped abruptly, sheathed them, and bowed. 'I found these upstairs.'

She waved her palm in front of her face. 'I'd give it five minutes if I were you.'

He opened the pork scratchings and began chewing. Sabre was instantly by his side, tail brushing the floorboards, unsettling dust balls. 'Are they sharp enough?' Jason patted his rifle. 'I'd rather trust this.'

She took a long slug of her drink, wiped her mouth on the back of her sleeve, was about to take a pork scratching but remembered her few teeth, then walked to the bar door, one side hanging off its hinges. 'Only one way to find out.' She stuck her head outside, put two fingers in her mouth and let out a long and loud wolf whistle that would make a builder on scaffolding proud.

Sabre gave a whine and put a paw on Jason's knee.

Jason tossed a few of the pork treats on the floor for him, sighed, then picked up his rifle and stood at the ready.

A plump woman in a tattered floral dress burst through the doorway. Her red eyes spotted Imogen and lunged for her.

Imogen swayed to her left and drew the swords in one swift movement. Her right arm swung in the air towards the woman, her sword delved into her neck and, with a small amount of resistance, cut her head clean off. It slammed down the infected woman's breasts, then bounced twice across to the bar, as if thirsty, then rested against the highly polished brass footrest that ran the length of the counter. The body crumpled forward and Imogen sliced through its abdomen, hacking aside the cotton dress, exposing flesh and then guts which flopped out in a steaming pile by Imogen's feet.

Sabre was up and skating across the polished floor and scrambled to an indignant rest by the fresh offal as the woman's liver flopped out and wobbled across the sausage-like pile, then slide to a rest on the floor.

'Leave,' shouted across Jason as he took a few steps forward, gagging as he went.

Imogen brought the blades nearer to her face. For a closer inspection, 'I'd say they were sharp.' She picked up a rough amount of the woman's dress, exposing her thighs, wiped the blades and expertly re-sheathed them. Turning to Jason, she put her hands together, fingers splayed as if in prayer, then bowed to him again.

The colonel's eye stopped twitching. His mouth was agape. He leant with his right hand on the back of the operator's chair and moved his head nearer to the screen, tilting the operator forwards as he peered at the camera feed. He finally whispered, 'What a killing machine.'

Chapter 16

The red and white coverings of the market stall flapped in the breeze. Bits of paper were scattered along the Market Square, along with stall contents and bodies. Lots of bodies. It had been a busy farmer's market. Shopping bags laid discarded; food contents were scattered. Individually wrapped pies, joints of beef and pork and wax wrapped cheeses were scattered on the tarmac, like a game of food chess. Some of their wrappers had been torn open, probably by beaks, and their inners eaten.

'Are you keeping them?' Jason nodded to her shoulders.

Imogen grinned. 'Too right!' Her pistol was holstered and her rifle slung to her side. Her hands were by her shoulders, ready to whip up to her new toys. Weapons that only she had. She'd long forgotten about the grenades.

The awnings of the other stalls did little to protect the stall holders. It looked like the infected had turned quickly here and helped themselves to what the traders had to offer: their blood. The smell was overwhelming. Faces had small holes in them, as if rats had found their way and been nibbling. They probably had, along with seagulls and other large birds. A few were missing their eyeballs. Jason wondered if they had been sucked like large gobstoppers or swallowed whole. He shuddered at the thought of the eyes popping in mouths, thick slime dribbling out. 'We can't help here. Let's check the surrounding shops and get back to the Land Rover.'

Imogen fingered the hilts of her swords, scanning the area for any infected. She was disappointed. She helped herself to several packets of oatcakes, throwing some down for Sabre to keep him from licking the crusted blood that covered the area.

Jason picked up and sniffed at some cheese, then slung it back, uneaten, onto the table. He crossed the road, towards a bank and a row of coffee shops. He could murder a black coffee, hot and steaming, thick with caffeine. The Cola sugar rush hadn't revived him, nor slaked his thirst. Chairs and tables were scattered, cups, saucers and plates were strewn around the pavement. The seagulls had eaten the scattered food. They must have had their fill, for the faces here were not pecked. 'Anyone alive? Come on out. We'll guide you to safety,' he yelled as he turned on the spot, willing survivors to crawl out from their hiding places. The town remained silent. He looked up at the flats above the shops. An old gold-painted sign, for a haberdashery, had been exposed during renovation work and left as a historic feature. Its bright calligraphy lettering beamed down on the square. Below it was a well-stocked pharmacy that hadn't been looted. Imogen showed no interest in going inside.

A window in the flats above was suddenly thrust open. A thin young male poked his head out. 'Hey man, where is everybody?' He peered down at the duo and their dog, his long, greasy hair dangling down, like Rapunzel's from the tower. He brought up a bong to his mouth and took a long draft. A wide smile brightened his face, accentuating his thin cheek bones. 'Not that I care. It's so quiet. I feel like I've slept for days after taking a line.' He sniffed deeply and felt along his nose. 'Want some?' he offered, waving the thick multi-coloured device with the wide base and elongated stem that looked phallic. He took another draw from the side tube that jutted out about two inches from the bottom. Puffs of smoke drifted away from him in the breeze.

A distant memory and a strong yearning filled Imogen's mind, and she struggled with a desire to join the young man. She opted to tickle Sabre under the chin instead, bringing her back to the present, and fingered around her chest rig pouch, to where her green liquid was safely in its bottle.

'Don't worry, man, I'm going for another lie down.' The head bobbed back indoors, and the window was then shut, and the curtains pulled tight in a deft movement.

Imogen shrugged, then gave a shrill whistle to attract anyone else, living, or infected. No one came obediently to her. She spotted a mini supermarket and strolled over, clucking for Sabre to follow. The automatic door was wedged open by a body. She jumped over it, walked to the till, helped herself to a bag for life, then found the pet aisle and chose the most expensive tinned dog meat, along with a box of gravy bones. She joined Jason on the pavement and put the bag down. 'I'll pick it up later when we've the Land Rover.'

He pointed to a weather-worn, dull brown painted building. It matched the colour of the innocent's blood that plastered and dried in the Market Square. The old building towered over the Market Square, as if watching over it. Its tall windows revealed it was built in an age of oil lamps and every inch of natural light was needed. The third floor would make a great vantage point. 'We'll come back to that hotel before nightfall, and find a room. I think we should sleep together, the three of us. For safety.'

She nodded. She knew she'd not want to sleep alone, not for some time yet.

'Let's get back to the Land Rover. The town is big. I think we need to explore the residential houses and flats. If I was a survivor, I'd make for home. Unless the colonel rings beforehand.'

They both looked up to the skies. The grey clouds, matching their moods, didn't step aside to reveal a drone, watching them, with thermal imaging and live streaming back to the officer.

Jason looked down at Sabre, he was matted in blood again. 'Change of plan. Let's clean our lad up first.' Pointing at the side of the hotel, he revealed, 'There is a car park there, and it leads directly to the sea. There's lots of shingle, then the ocean. That'll clean our boy up.' He led the way back to their vehicle.

Sabre jumped from the Land Rover, spun on the spot in excitement, and went hurtling off. The dog jumped over the walkway that led walkers to the distant harbour and bounded onto the shingle. This made him falter as his paws tentatively walked over the various sized rocks and stones. He rolled over and over an enormous pile of seaweed, still black from the sea. It kept its wet and salty goodness and he rubbed his muzzle deep into the pile, burrowing within strands and ribbons, then fell forward and rolled again, instinctively knowing how to rub down his coat, ridding himself of the infected blood.

Laughter broke out as Imogen and Jason watched him, their minds far from the killings. They simply lived in the moment, carefree for just a few minutes as they watched Sabre bolt for the sea and leap between the shingle and the ebb and flow of the tide. The dog was soon swimming in circles, one eye on his tribe, the other relishing getting clean. He broke from the surface and ran to his owners, coming to a halt by their boots. He shook himself dry.

Giggling, Imogen, and Jason turned away, drying their faces from the splattered sea water, not caring that their combat uniform was getting wet. The sea water droplets did little to remove the caked blood.

Imogen was the first to look up. Her eyes narrowed as she squinted from the glare of the sun. She was looking towards the car park in the distance that led to the start of the walkway path that skirted the beach and ran the length of the rear of the houses and shops they'd recently passed. She pointed in the other direction and Jason followed to where she was staring. 'Lend me your binoculars, Cowboy. I think I see a seal bobbing in the water. I've never seen one close. They are rather cute.'

Jason unwound them from his neck, passing them to her as he peered into the sea. 'I can't see one. Mind you, I've seen loads over the years. Pippa and I used to go to Torry Battery with a flask of coffee and some cakes. My binoculars at home are more powerful than these. Sometimes we'd see dolphins. I wonder if we still have a home to go back to. I hope so.' His voice trailed off.

Wanting to take his mind off his thoughts and what she'd seen behind them, she asked, 'I'd like to see dolphins. Perhaps take me there one day?' She bent to the shingle and picked up a stick, about the length and thickness of an arm.

'Sure. It'll be a good place to camp out. There shouldn't be many infected there, as it's far enough from most houses and other buildings. The deserted fort will shelter us from the elements and it'll be an excellent defensive position. We can pitch up for the night. It'll be nice to see the sunset over the sea.' He took the offered branch; the bark had dried out in the sun long ago and been stripped by the sea. It looked bleached. 'What's this for?'

'Throw it out to sea for Sabre. He needs to go in deeper and have a wash. He's still got blood on his coat.'

'Okay.' Jason went wandering off down the beach, whistling sharply to the dog. 'What's this, boy?' he teased, waving it in the air like a baton to get the dog's attention.

Imogen lifted the binoculars and peered out to sea, then casually looped around to the pathway where two groups of men and women were running towards each other, like two armies on a Scottish glen, proudly fighting for their clans. Some carried gardening tools like hoes and spades, outstretched in their arms, like lances. Others had cricket bats, while one wore the remnants of a Police Scotland uniform and was wielding a baton. The group sprinting from the car park was now facing Imogen and she could see their red eyes and blood-stained mouths and fronts. They were heading her way, but first they had to plough through the group twenty metres from them and closing.

The two groups converged in a mix of gnashing teeth and cavorting limbs. Blows were exchanged and bladed garden tools were thrust through flesh. Muscles and sinews were gouged out and fresh blood poured from gaping wounds. The crowd thinned and as the converging men and women who had their backs to her twisted and fell, she could see their red, infected eyes. The zombies were turning on each other. 'Damn, that's less for me to have fun with.' She made do with vicarious violence instead and nodded approvingly as two twenty-year-olds bit deep into each other's necks, as if they were horny teenagers and declaring their love openly by leaving love bites. They fell to the ground wrapped in each other's arms, neither wanting to relinquish their hold, dying from the blood loss that gushed onto the wooden path, staining the wood permanently.

One teenager was pierced in the stomach by a long hoe that was thrust at a run. It skewered him. His assailant lifted him up in the air and Imogen sucked air through her few remaining teeth at the sight and made a mental note to visit the hardware shop she'd spotted earlier. The victim floundered in the air, like a turtle lifted from the sea, then was thrown into the melee. His body knocked over two old ladies, their cardigans heavy with thick, congealed blood, weighing them down. They were trampled to death as eager feet stamped into them to reach opponents. Their numbers thinned until just one survivor victoriously looked around, needing to feed, but finding no one alive. He headed off towards the harbour, nose sniffing in the air. Imogen wished she had The Long to hand.

Pointing to the north, away from the battle, Jason gleefully said, 'I'll take you to see the best fish and chip shop in Stonehaven. Probably the finest in Scotland, certainly the number one chipper in Aberdeenshire. It's won awards.'

'Did they get a badge for it?' she sarcastically asked as she turned and walked with him. Not bothering him about the latest sight. He'd only worry.

'Oh, yes, and lots of certificates to display on the walls between their branded mugs and special bags to keep your chips warm. Pippa and I bought one. Our wrapped fish suppers keep hot for ages in them.' He sighed, reliving the happy memories as he strolled off.

Sabre followed. The dog dived amongst the grass and shingle that bordered the path and began sniffing furiously. He then crouched and voided a long held in bowel movement. Nobody came behind him with a small plastic bag with handles. He turned around and sniffed at what came out of him, then bounded after his mistress and master.

They soon reached a small street that narrowed into a promenade. Chairs and tables were strewn across the pavement and road. Several bodies laid on the tarmac with pools of dried blood surrounding them, like a dull-red outline. The brightly coloured ice-cream and sweet shop, named after someone's favourite aunty, seemed to mock the sombre scene. Its awning flapped in the wind, as if waving at the duo, enticing them in. Neither of the pair went to check if any of the bodies were still alive. Their purple features gave away how long they'd laid there after taking their last frightened, struggling breath.

'You wouldn't believe the size of the ice-creams you'd get from here,' boasted Jason. 'Massive cones, filled to the brim. As if that wasn't enough, they'd layer in chocolates, flakes, wafers, marshmallows, and chewy sweets. It was a diabetic consultant's worse nightmare.' He licked his lips at the memory. 'But super tasty. Especially on a hot day.' He looked wistfully away towards the sea. 'It was a favourite day away for Pippa and me.'

Imogen walked into the small shop and glanced at the deep trays boasting various flavours of ice-cream. Each was runny, with foul cream floating to the top. There was a sour smell in the air. She leapt over the counter and grabbed at various jars. She began emptying half-filled ones into a large one that dominated the service counter. She had a child-like excitement in her eyes. 'We'll definitely be parking up here before we bed down for the night.' Fizzy flying saucers were being scooped into her new booty.

'Is it safe to come out?' whispered a female voice.

Imogen spun around, pulling out her right sword. She dropped a jar of pineapple cubes. It spilled on the floor, scattering yellow squares across the linoleum. Several were crunched under the feet of an emerging teenager from under the sink area. She had been hiding in a small cupboard. 'Show me your eyes,' demanded Imogen.

The young girl, about nineteen, hair astray, wearing a creased tunic with the shop's logo, blinked several times as she got used to the light. 'My eyes?' She asked in puzzlement.

'No matter, I can see you are not infected.' Imogen put away her sword and reached out for a jar of white chocolate discs that were coated in hundreds and thousands. She began munching away. Her eyes seemed to twinkle as the flavours hit her tongue.

'People started fighting. I hid in the cleaning cupboard. It was a tight fit. I'd been scrubbing the toilets with strong bleach. I hate doing it because the ammonia can set off my allergies, even if I wear a mask and gloves. The owner has a thing about the staff toilets being super clean in case the environmental health inspectors come on a surprise visit. He hates them. You should hear him curse at the Aberdeenshire Council staff. They are super picky and always leave him with a long list of things to do. They should go to some of the other shops in this area. We are super clean and our food hygiene is top-notch.' She stood up straight and proud.

Imogen let her warble on. She'd spotted the fizzy laces and was busy stuffing several strands into her mouth. She turned and gave the jar a shake in Jason's direction. It looked like wriggling worms were coming out of her mouth.

He shook his head. 'You're hyper enough as it is. That sugar rush is going to have you bouncing from the walls!'

She grinned, and red saliva drooled from her mouth and oozed down her chin. She grabbed a nearby paper napkin and dried herself, and allowed the soiled tissue to drop on the floor.

The shop assistant watched in disgust, tutted loudly, walked over, and began picking up the discarded rubbish. 'Are you the police? You look military. Why the guns?' her forehead wrinkled when she noticed Imogen's swords.

'For our and your protection. People are still fighting and trying to kill each other. Can you drive?'

She nodded. 'But I don't have a license. I keep failing my test.'

Jason grinned. 'That's the least of your problems. Let's find you a vehicle.'

She followed him out and watched as he stooped over a thick-set man with a large Groucho Marx type moustache. She gave a little scream. He was dressed in a leather waistcoat which was adorned with various metal badges. It must have been heavy to wear. Jason turned him over and delved into his jeans pocket, and pulled out a key. Parked a few feet away was a three-wheeled motorbike with a deep chair and wide handlebars. It was the only vehicle in this pedestrianised area. 'You figure you can drive this?'

She shrugged. 'I guess so. But where do I go? Can I go home now? Will me and my family be safe?'

'You sure that's wise, Cowboy? There's no protection from running and jumping infected,' warned Imogen.

Jason looked around. There were no other vehicles. 'Go as fast as you can. This beauty looks like it was built for speed. Stop for nothing. Don't go home. Pray your family made it out alive. Make for Dundee, stop at the fence that crosses the road. The military will take you to safety. They'll help you find your family.'

'Fence? Across the main road? The A90? Both carriageways?'

'Yes. This region has been quarantined. There's been an outbreak.'

'Like a disease?' she asked. Her mouth hanging open.

'Something like that.' He handed her the keys and knelt by the motorbike, rifle at the ready, in anticipation of the infected bursting out at the noise of the engine.

She sat astride the behemoth, looking like a rag doll driving a tricycle. She gunned the throttle, and

Sabre whined at the noise, his ears moving from side to side, his head tilting. The teenager tore down the road, screaming in terror as she went. Her cries echoed around the surrounding cafes and Jason's favourite fish and chip takeaway, then subsided, along with the distant engine noise. He hadn't the heart to take Imogen into the brightly nautical-blue painted building. He didn't want to see another of Pippa's favourite places fall to destruction.

'She'll crash,' quipped Imogen. 'She doesn't have a clue how to handle something that powerful between her legs!'

Chapter 17

The acrid, salty smell of sea water mingled with blood hit the trio as they entered the open-air swimming pool. Sabre's nose was working overtime as it twitched away, almost in time to the lapping water as fresh sea water came in and sluiced away more blood from the multitude of floating bodies. They were bobbing about like inquisitive seals in a harbour, awaiting a trawler to empty the fish guts overboard.

Jason crouched, his hand over his eyes. His shoulders shuddering as sobs escaped him. He felt a warm hand on his shoulder. It rubbed at his exposed neck. 'There are so many children. So many innocents. They didn't deserve this.' Snot and phlegm tore from him and he blew it away onto the red-tiled floor. 'No one we've seen over the last two days does.'

Imogen whispered back, 'I know, I know.' She looked around at the art deco styled open-air swimming pool with bold themes of blue pillars and yellow facings on the building and benches around the sides. The water was a deep blue, stained red in places with the blood and flesh of victims that the tide inlet hadn't quite reached. Brightly coloured umbrellas, protection from the sun for the bathers, fluttered in the breeze, the wind crack breaking the solemn silence. Streams of bunting stretched across the skyline of the pool, as if mocking the deaths by their bright, cheerful hues. The Olympic size pool housed dozens of floating corpses doing impersonations of still backstrokes and front crawls, save for the ebb and flow from the sea water inlet. The odd floating device bobbed among the corpses. Several of the toddlers wore inflated arm floats, giving them the illusion of plastic muscles.

Red and blue ropes floated down the length of the pool, marking the swimming lanes. They bobbed as fresh sea water continued to make its way into the pool. The inlet was no longer heating it for the comfort of the swimmers. There was no comfort here. One rope had been wrapped around a swimmer. His tongue protruding from his bulging eyes and he was bloated, making his face puffy. He bobbed up and down, like a marker buoy at sea.

A long yellow slide was blocked with the bodies of several girls, their bikinis not needed to cover their inadequate breasts, giving away their young age. They looked like they'd been frozen in time, sliding down, except there was no fun etched into their grimacing faces. The adjoining blue steps were crowded with the corpses of hairless boys who had been crushed in their frantic endeavours to escape the lifeguard, who had swiftly turned on them and had bitten deep into the first few necks. It looked like the lifeguard had tripped on a step and had broken his neck.

'Turn away Jason, we can't help here. Guard my approach. I'll quickly check the changing rooms.' She unsheathed her two swords and had them at the ready as she entered a yellow-tiled room with rows of red lockers. Towels were strewn on the floor and were of no use to the near naked corpses whose blood had drained conveniently down the small gutters built into the tiles. She approached the changing room, small cubicles, painted a garish red to match the victims, and pulled open each wooden door. They were empty. She allowed them to bang shut, not caring about breaching the silence of this near mortuary like room.

The other changing room was the same. Even the shocked frozen expressions of the women bathers matched those of the men. The infected must have ripped them apart before the chemical attack infected them. Imogen wasn't sure which fate was worse. The turnstiles and enclosed area made this a perfect killing ground for the infected, and it must have happened quickly. Several of the dead had blood stains down their mouths and necks, so they must have turned on each other within seconds.

There was no last look around as she left. Her job here was done. 'Let's leave here,' she sighed as she returned to Jason, who was looking around at the carnage, checking for any of the infected.

Pointing to the floating corpses he croaked out, 'We can't just leave them. It seems wrong. Disrespectful.'

'I know. But it's not our job to clean up. We've been tasked with finding survivors or kill the infected. We aren't the burial party.'

He shivered. 'The graves will be endless. Hazlehead Crematorium will also have to work around the clock. Mass graves will have to be dug. It's unthinkable.'

'Then don't. Think about it, I mean,' she insisted as she took his hand and led him away.

'The bodies are bloating, blackening, and smelling. It'll be horrific picking them up. Some might even liquify.'

She took a few steps forward, almost dragging him away. 'It's not our problem. Harsh as it sounds.' Imogen stopped and looked him straight in the eye. 'I need you to focus on the here and now. Our mission is to save or kill. Not bury nor fret. Do you hear me?'

He nodded, then shook his head clear. 'I'll get through that fence they've built. I need to get to Pippa and our baby.'

'Good. Then let's go.'

He strode purposefully back to the ornate Victorian turnstiles that barred the entrance and leapt over them. Sabre following, his mighty legs taking them in one bound.

She turned; glad he hadn't seen the one-year-old that had been dragging itself out from beneath its mother's corpse. Its red eyes glowing sharply against the dull red flooring. It had been making its way to them. Imogen pulled out her Glock 19, then immediately holstered it again. She wanted a silent kill. Jason didn't need to know about this one. She pulled out a sword, a sullen look on her face, and walked towards it and slashed, making it quick. She took no pleasure in watching the head roll and splash into the pool, like a rogue, rolling beach ball in the wind. Imogen looked down at the headless body, then at the pool. A tear dropped from her eye. 'I'm sorry.'

Chapter 18

Jason looked at the phone, willing the colonel to ring. He'd tried the only number stored on the mobile, but it went unanswered. He watched as Imogen strolled down the yellow steps of the swimming pool entrance. The two flags above the tall columned doorway fluttered impotently in the still wind, reflecting his feelings of helplessness. He tried not to look at the bodies that were sprawled across the yellow railings of the disabled access ramp. But his eyes were drawn to them. They looked like marionettes in a macabre performance as they just hung there, ready for someone to animate them. A pool of blood had dripped, seeped, and dried down to the brickwork. 'We are the cause of many of the bodies that will need to be cleared by someone. Probably the military. It's the stuff of nightmares. We've doubtlessly caused the clean-up squad their PTSD.'

'Snap out of it!' shouted Imogen. 'You are no use to me like this.'

He stared at her and remained silent. A chastised schoolboy.

Sabre whined.

'Sorry,' he whispered after a few awkward moments. 'I know they aren't people anymore. Fucking Russians. I hope they pay for this.'

'We need to do our own plan of action. Forget the colonel and his thermal imaging. Where is the next populated area?'

He looked around him. 'The caravan park. It's peak holiday season for the English and overseas tourists. Our schools in Scotland went back a week ago, I think. But the schools in England have a different timetable. They broke up later. The caravan park would have been busy.'

'Good, that's helpful. We need to clear this town and get back to the fence and near to Pippa. Keep that in your mind.'

He nodded furiously. 'I doubt many would have been wearing masks. They wouldn't be doing any DIY, like I was doing when the Russian plane attacked. Nor holding up a shop like you,' he quipped.

Her face reddened, and her smile was broad. 'A girl's got to make an honest living.'

He laughed; her toothless grin always cheered him up. 'What a team we make. I'm glad it's you I've been partnered with. And Sabre, of course.' He tickled the dog's ears.

Sabre stroked his muzzle against Jason's thigh, relishing the attention.

Imogen's toothy grin broadened further and her sallow, thin face stretched as it tried to puff out in pride. 'Let's go, before you get even soppier. You drive, Cowboy.'

'Up, up,' he commanded Sabre, and pointed to the back of the Land Rover. The dog bounded over and leapt, then settled amongst the discarded clothing and mounds of brass bullet casings.

Jason made a mental note to find him a duvet from a hotel or a plusher bed from a pet store.

'There must be someone. It's a big town. It was bustling with tourists up to yesterday morning,' complained the colonel to the still room.

None of the screen operators answered him. They were growing more and more alarmed at his outbursts and erratic behaviour.

The Stonehaven screen operator tensed her shoulders. They'd only been here two days and one night, but it felt like two weeks. The watching was intense. The sights she'd witnessed were appalling. Each encounter was getting ghastlier. She couldn't help a shudder.

The colonel strode to the other side of the Ops Room. 'Get the drone to sweep past again. Slower this time. There must be survivors in this section.'

A caravan door swung open and a middle-aged man in a polo shirt and shorts fell down the three steps. He squirmed on the grass and righted himself. His red eyes looking around him, as if he was in a haze.

A sword spliced through the air and sliced through his throat. Imogen stood back as blood poured out, staining the grass.

The corpse fell flat on its face, twitching twice, and then remained still, save for the blood seeping into the earth.

'That's for blocking the roads with your stupid mobile home from homes.'

'Not a fan of caravan holidays, then?' jibed Jason.

'No. Why can't they get a hotel room, like everyone else?'

Jason crouched on one knee, taking aim with his SA80. 'You ever been on one?' He shot a running man clean through the neck.

The man ran another two faltering steps, then fell in a heap.

'God, no!'

'Then how do you know they aren't fun? My parents took me on many static caravan holidays. It was great fun. There are lots to do for youngsters.'

A go-kart, made to look like a Formula 1 racing car, came belting down the road. It flew over the speed bump, its occupant flying into the air momentarily, before setting back into its seat. Its snarling mouth wasn't making Jason and Imogen feel welcome.

Still standing at the entrance to the caravan and camping site, by the hut-like reception building with an assortment of flags above the roof, Imogen turned to Jason. 'I'll handle the children.'

'Thank you,' he murmured. He turned away as Imogen whipped out her catapult and put a ball bearing clean through the youngster's forehead.

His head jerked back, then he slumped over his steering wheel, forcing the go-kart to career into the side of a pitched tent. The nylon fabric collapsed in on itself, burying the boy and his toy vehicle.

The incident reminded Imogen of a Beano cartoon strip. She half expected Dennis the Menace to come round the corner with Gnasher. Seeing Jason's solemn face, she remained silent and didn't share the joke. 'Let's check the place out.'

They started by a small row of trees where there was a grassed area interspersed with gravel parking. The spaces were big enough to hold the largest of motorhomes. Most had cables running to a post at the rear. Several had portable whirly gig washing lines that looked like miniature tripod machines from the War of the Worlds. Others had cumbersome satellite dishes, bringing their favourite channels, if there was any power to this region. The duo, with their dog, entered each home, taking it in turns to wait outside each narrow entrance. Most were empty. The occupants had made the most of the fine weather and had gone into town. Or the nearby swimming pool.

Pistol at the ready, Jason mounted the middle motorhome and immediately entered the dark kitchen. He could make out breakfast dishes, two bowls of spilt corn flakes. The milk smelled rancid. He opened a door which revealed a small cupboard; no humans were hiding within. He glanced across to the lounge area with its plush corner sofa and deep cushions. It was clear. He strolled over, pulled out a cushion and held it out, imagining measuring if it was suitable for Sabre.

The door leading to the bedrooms and bathroom sprung open, and a man dressed in boxer shorts ran out. His chest was caked in blood, the colour matching his eyes. He leapt across to Jason, causing them both to fall back against a wooden table. It collapsed with the weight of them, Jason's rear ammo pouches taking the brunt of the impact. The weight of the man was fully on him and he struggled against the snarling and air biting that came perilously close to his cheek. He turned away, neck muscles straining. As the man was wrapping his hands around Jason's throat, Jason wriggled and brought his hand around, aimed the pistol and shot through the cushion. The force of the Glock 19 bullet instantly burrowing through the fabric, found the man's chest, and exited through his back. The infected man was thrown backwards, hitting his head on the back of one of the open-air kitchen cabinets, snapping his neck, severing his spine, just as he was bleeding out.

Jason sprang to his feet, pistol raised, running through to the bedrooms and bathroom. No living was there. He left the dead where they were. On his way out, he picked up a sealed jar of hotdogs. As he was walking down the steps, he unhooked the cushion from where it was tucked tightly under his armpit. He passed it and the hotdogs to Imogen.

Holding it up to the air, she shook her head. 'Nope. It's got a hole in it.' She nodded to where she heard the gunshot. 'Get another one.' Patting the dog on the head and feeding him a hotdog, she retorted, 'Only the best for my boy!'

Jason shook his head and returned to the scene of his crime.

Chapter 19

The roar of engines broke into the silence and a convoy of quad bikers screeched to a halt by the red and white pole barrier of the caravan and camping site. A youth jumped off his green and black machine, ran to the barrier, pushing it forward, grunting with exertion. It yielded after a few seconds and bent forward, giving his mates room to pass. They cheered and waved, like they were on a racetrack and exciting the crowd before an event. The youth ran back to his vehicle, revved up, and drove after them. His long hair flapped in the wind. No one wore helmets. They weren't worried about being stopped by the police. His mates were nearing Jason and Imogen.

'Sabre, sit,' ordered Jason as he saw the convoy, now three deep, spread across the road, blocking any passage. He raised his hands for them to halt.

The youths accelerated, driving around them in threatening circles.

Sabre was growling, hackles raised, looking between this new threat and Jason. Yearning for a fresh command.

'Fuck this,' hissed Imogen as she raised her SA80 and let out a stream of bullets. Several thudded and bounced off two of the quad bikes' metalwork.

High-pitched screams erupted and one youngster, about fifteen, jumped from his vehicle and rolled onto the grass. He thudded into a caravan while his bike came to a careering halt in some bushes. The engine groaned in protest and spluttered out. 'I surrender, I surrender!' he screamed at them, rising to his feet, arms high in the air.

The others came to a halt and turned off their engines. Jumping from their vehicles, they too raised their hands in the air. 'Are you the army?' the oldest asked in a tentative voice.

'Yes,' replied Imogen. 'What the fuck are you lot doing? You are putting yourself at risk.'

'You could have shot us, killed us,' he exclaimed in a high-pitched voice. 'We are only having fun. We were having a track day on my father's field yesterday.

It gets dusty, so we had our face scarfs on under our helmets and visors. Mum insists we wear them. She checks on us.' He continued in a low voice, 'I found her body, next to my father's. They had been attacked. Murdered.' He shivered. 'We don't know what's going on, but we've been running down anyone who looks like a crazy zombie. We've spent yesterday and today going to each other's farms to look for family and friends. No one is alive. Well, not normal. The crazies have red eyes. Did our masks protect us? We saw the yellow smoke from the strange plane that flew past us. Is it a zombie apocalypse?' he questioned, mispronouncing the last word.

'Yes,' replied Imogen. 'It's the end of days. For this region anyway.' She raised her weapon. 'Leave the killing for us experts.'

Several of the youths took a step back, and there were generalised mutterings of confusion.

Jason broke it with a shout. 'Listen up. Get back on your quads and make for Dundee. This isn't a game. Go as fast as you safely can and don't stop for anyone. Try to go around them, it'll be safer for you.

Stop at a big fence, you can't miss it. There will be military there who will explain things and get you to safety.'

A heavy-set teenager, biceps honed from years of helping his family around the farm, stepped forward. 'No way, man. My parents were murdered. I want justice.'

Imogen walked up to him. She lifted her rifle and thrust its muzzle under his chin. 'Don't get in our way, pal. Do as you are told, or I'll slot you.'

The road turned wet and a damp patch appeared on his trouser groin and down his leg. He stuttered, 'Okay. Sorry. But kill them. Kill them all. I've played Farmers versus Zombies on my PlayStation. We can help.'

'Can you fuck?' she hissed. 'As if playing computer games will train you for reality, for a zombie haven.'

Jason chuckled and rolled his eyes. 'If only they knew,' he whispered to Sabre.

The dog cocked his ears, and his hackles receded. He'd given up the growling seconds earlier.

Imogen gave Jason a silencing look, turned back to the youth, and pushed the muzzle deeper into his neck. 'Now get to fuck.'

The group ran to their machines, like Spitfire pilots scrambled for The Battle of Britain. They throttled their engines, spun, and wheeled out of the caravan park, not stopping to aid their friend to get his quad bike from the bushes. He was left to yank it out from the undergrowth and high-tailed it out by himself. He looked like the unfit soldier who always lagged at the end of a squad run, hobbling in front of the trailing ambulance, ready to drive him back to the barracks medical centre when the physical training instructor had enough of shouting at him.

'Stupid fuckers, they'll get themselves, or us, killed,' spat Imogen. 'Got to admire their balls, though. They are lucky to have survived.'

They turned away and walked through the campsite, looking for the infected, hoping for survivors.

More of the infected were bustling by the campsite dedicated to smaller tents. They were squatting down on their haunches in the middle of the central grass. It reminded Jason of a Scouts campfire, without the logs burning away in the middle. Or the cheerful singing. Instead, there was a sinister low hum emanating from the group.

Faces turned in their direction, noses raised in the air, sniffing the approach of fresh meat. Several sprang from crouching and began running towards Jason. He shot them with a quick spray of bullets. They danced in the air, throwing their limbs akimbo, as if at a ham seventies disco revival. Then they fell.

Imogen ran to the group, drawing her swords as she sprinted, jumping over a guide rope that secured the first tent. As she landed, she swiped down her sword, taking a head clean off the shoulders before the undead could stand. Hands reached for her and found her chest rig, forcing her down. She dropped her swords and thrust her knee into the unfeeling groin of her assailant. 'Fucker! That usually floors them.' She pulled out a small combat knife and plunged it into the snarling face, slicing clean through a cheek, exposing teeth and gums. Its awkward angle missed the bone, and she drove it home by hitting it with her palm, forcing it into the brain. She felt the body shudder, like they were making love and he'd just climaxed. Then it released his grip and dropped.

Sabre sprinted forward and bit down on the nearest ankle and started shaking. Another body fell, and he began ripping and biting its face, arms, any exposed flesh, until it was still. With blood dripping from his fangs, he chose another victim and took a run, then jump and bit down on an arm that was instinctively raised in protection. It didn't afford any and was soon pouring out blood. It sprayed tents as it was shaken; the liquid running down the waterproof fabric.

An SA80 rifle spat out carefully aimed bullets as Jason warily chose targets away from the dog and Imogen. He watched until they dropped, then aimed for another. He was unaware of the young woman approaching him from behind until her arms were around his chest, squeezing. His chest rig prevented her from doing any damage, but the surprise attack made him drop his rifle. He tried twisting and turning, but she held on firm. Then he lent forward, hoping to throw his assailant over his shoulders. Instead, she used this momentum to jump on him. She wrapped her legs around his waist and straddled him, like they were a couple at a music festival and she wanted a better look at the band.

'Having fun?' asked a breathless Imogen, stooped over, catching her breath after her battle.

'A bit of help,' he pleaded while trying to keep his attacker from biting into his exposed neck. He whirled around and around.

Imogen rolled her eyes and shouted, 'Stand still, you silly bugger!'

He obliged and Imogen grabbed the woman, a thin-looking twenty-year-old. Her slight frame allowed Imogen to pull her off Jason and throw her to the ground. The surprise of the fall gave Imogen enough time to reach for her bloodied sword and, as the woman knelt to steady herself, Imogen chopped through her neck. The blunted sword caught on the spinal column and got stuck. The woman collapsed as her neck and head peeled open, the weight of her body caused the sword to snap in two. 'Bollocks!' exclaimed Imogen, at the loss of her weapon.

Jason spun around on the spot, pistol pulled out as he twisted around, looking for any other attacker. There was no one else. The caravan park was still except for the sound of their laboured breathing. 'Thanks,' came a breathless gratitude.

'You're welcome!' She mock curtsied, bending at the waist while pulling an imaginary dress hem to the sides.

He giggled. 'I guess I owe you a new weapon.'

'I guess you do. Let's clear the other side of the camp.' She pointed to rows of caravans. Most of the pitches had a large car beside them. As they neared, they could see that they differed in age. Some older caravans looked battered and less cared for. One had an assortment of town stickers on its window, proudly boasting about where it had visited and set up a pitch. Imogen drew out her other sword and gave a few practice swipes. It felt like she'd lost a limb and was having to relearn balance and to move about all over again. 'I have something in mind. Can we go back to town after clearing here?'

'Sure. I guess we have time.' The phone in his pocket hadn't vibrated or made any sound. He caught a strip of beef jerky she threw at him. He was loving the treats the ration packs had provided. He bit down, guilt-free as he could see Sabre had been given one too. He couldn't help but notice that it was larger.

Chapter 20

'I wouldn't bother. The meat will be rancid.' Jason shouted to Sabre, 'Sit. Stay.' He looked up at the butcher's shop, painted in the traditional red and white style, with an awning over the sign. A model of a well-fed butcher in a white apron jacket and a straw hat stood proudly outside. Its eyes were averted to the bodies sprawled inside.

The door was closed, but Imogen soon pushed it open. Then she took a step back as a waft of reeking meat assailed her nostrils. She could hear the gentle droning of flies. It was her turn to do the gagging. She pulled up her green snood from around her neck. She'd found it in the kitbag and thought it would shield her against bites. Now it gave her protection from the rancid odours as she pulled it over her mouth and nostrils. Entering the shop, she ignored the bodies, lying prone over a wicker-style shopping basket, curving the back of the woman, as if she was trying to hide her shopping from prying eyes. Imogen hopped onto the counter and swung her legs over and walked through the archway and into the meat preparation area. Bending over a dead butcher who had died clasping a large meat cleaver, she prised his fingers off it, ignoring the snapping bones. She then walked across to the large table and browsed casually at the implements. Grinning, she ambled around the area, pausing at the clothing pegs. She swiped away the flies that had already gathered to feast.

'Fourteen! That's fantastic, the most yet. I want them alive.' The colonel's eyes were alight with desire, and he began tapping out a text message. His twitching muscle beneath his left eye matched the tempo of his fingers. 'You did good. Well done.'

The young woman operating the CCTV networks beamed as she zoomed in on the large bungalow building, set in an extensive driveway with an ample car park. The plush, green grounds were a rare oasis of calm, with no bodies littering the grass. Birds fluttered down from the nearby trees and fed on the dwindling supply from the peanut holder that swung as they pecked. The operator took a moment to watch and take a calming breath. She hoped they'd bed down for the night and give her a rest from all the slaughter.

Jason, ignoring the beep, beep, of the phone, let out a laugh that echoed around the town square, disturbing the crows pecking away at the corpses just a few yards away. Sabre had been eyeing them attentively. 'What the fuck are you wearing now? You look like Sweeney Todd!'

Imogen tilted her straw hat and made chopping motions with her meat cleaver and her long filleting knife. 'Who the fuck's that?'

Shaking his head, he sighed, 'Never mind. Don't you trust your rifle?'

It was slung over her shoulder, opposite to her one remaining sword. A gleam entered her eye. 'This'll be more fun.'

Jason crouched on one knee. 'Here's your chance to try them out.' His rifle was aimed at a teenager running down the street. His sprinting legs were like pistons, forcing him on faster than his body wanted to go. His arms were swinging in the air, as if trying, fruitlessly, to slow himself down. His hoodie flapped against his head, the fabric on his chest was stiff with dried blood. 'Definitely infected.'

Imogen ran to meet him. Judging that he was taller than her, she leapt onto the bench to her left and bounced straight off it, using the momentum to gain height. As she curved back down, she raised both her hands and drove her weapons through his shoulders. The blades dug deep. Blood poured out and covered the memorial plaque screwed into the back of the bench, staining the wood. It splattered onto the pavement and was followed by two chunks of flesh that would have disgraced the skills of a master butcher. Two hewn arms flopped by Imogen's feet and the infected teenager ran several more steps before the loss of blood stopped his heart from working, and he fell flat to the floor. His face hitting the kerb, breaking his teeth and jaw. He came to rest by the back tyre of a parked car. The rubber halting his journey. 'Wow!' she exclaimed, breathless with exertion and excitement.

A sharp crack broke her admiring stare, and she heard a body crumple about twenty yards up the hill.

Jason rose from his crouch and then gave a scoffing curtsey. 'You're welcome!'

Imogen grinned, then wiping her blades clean, she inspected her handiwork and gave a low whistle of awe. Then she aimed the meat cleaver at Jason, and let it fly towards his head.

He ducked, just in time. He felt its keen edge slice through the air, parting his hair. It embedded into a wooden doorframe from which a young woman was emerging. She screamed, her clear-blue eyes staring wide at the sight of the bloodied uniform and knife wielding Imogen. She ran up the hill, shrieking like a banshee.

'Oops! I thought she was infected. Just as well I missed. Great throw, though, eh?' She ran after her, not waiting for a reply from Jason.

The phone was out and Jason shielded the screen from the sun and read the message. Walking up to where Imogen was bent over, panting, he ignored the nearby body and the blood that was flowing down the street, making its way into the street drain.

'She fell over and cracked her skull open. Sorry. Stupid cow, bursting out from behind you like that,' explained a breathless Imogen. She spat onto the pavement between gasping breaths.

He grimaced. He thought she looked like she was about to throw up. That would make a change from him, he pondered wryly. He shrugged. Death was becoming routine. It worried him. 'It was bound to have happened sooner or later. Our reactions will slow as we get more tired, poor lass. Blue-on-blue, we call it in the military.' He waved the mobile phone. 'We've a group in a nursing home, just up here. Let's get the Land Rover. You look knackered.'

They drove towards it at a cautious pace. Sabre was resting in the back, sulking at not being allowed to eat the tasty smelling meat in the last building Imogen had entered on her own.

Jason had his Glock 19 resting on his lap as he steered around the bend of the driveway. It was eerily silent, save for their engine noise. He turned in the car park and drove to the front door, not caring that he was blocking the road. He wanted a fast getaway if an infected crowd got too much.

Whistling for Sabre to wake up and join them, they walked the perimeter of the building. The windows were spotlessly clean, the bedrooms they peered in were empty. Most had a single bed, chests of drawers of various designs, probably taken from their former homes, and bedside tables that looked like those that adorned every hospital ward up and down the country. Two rooms had battered writing desks with leather tops and deep leather captain's chairs. A plush leather recliner graced another bedroom. A cable ran from a remote-control unit resting on the seat to an electric socket.

Imogen shrugged as they rounded another side, which revealed a gigantic washing machine and industrial drying machines. Piles of sheets with yellowing stains were scattered on the floor, spilling out of large white bags secured to a metal frame on wheels. She wrinkled her nose instinctively. 'You sure we are in the right place?'

Jason nodded and jumped as a hand banged on the massive windows with closed red curtains. A sign had been sellotaped to the inside glass. It simply said 'Help' in large letters. A head was peeking out from the curtains. Then a hand pointed to his right. He allowed himself to be led to a patio door and a window to the side of it opened a fraction.

'Have you come to rescue us?'

'That's right,' replied Imogen gleefully. 'We are the cavalry.' She grinned at Jason, 'Aren't we, Cowboy?'

The curtain was pulled back a fraction more, and a frown appeared on the young woman's face. She was dressed in a one-piece lilac dress with two pockets in the front. Her narrow breast pocket held two pens, one red, one black, and to the side of it was a white plastic fob watch. 'You don't look like the police.'

'We aren't.' Jason delved under his shirt and took out his rank slide lanyard and showed it to her.

Her frown deepened. 'I don't know what that is.'

Imogen laughed. 'You've just been demoted, Cowboy!'

Jason gave her a withering look and turned back to the carer. 'Are your patients alive? Our thermal imaging has captured fourteen of you. Though I'm told you aren't in the same rooms.'

She nodded vigorously. 'The manager started smashing the place up. It's not like her at all. She's normally so calm and patient. She's been ever so kind to me. Especially when my dad died. She has a lovely way with the patients, especially those with Alzheimer's. She's locked in her office. There are two bedbound patients, though I've had to lock them in their rooms as they tried to bite me when I tried to turn them. They'll be at risk of pressure sores.'

A tutting noise escaped from Jason. 'That'll be the least of their concerns.' He pointed to the patio door. 'Can you let us in, please?'

'It's locked. We have patients who wander. They have dementia, so can't be safely on their own outside. The manager has the key. I've been too frightened to get it from her.'

Jason sized up the window. 'Okay. Open this as far as you can. We'll squeeze in.'

'I've entered smaller windows than that,' declared Imogen proudly.

'I bet you have,' sighed Jason, wondering what riches she had nicked and sold over the years to feed her former habit. He hoped she wouldn't be tempted by the drugs that were bound to be held on these premises. He needed her focused.

The window cranked open, and the curtains were pulled back a few metres. 'I've been keeping these closed. Some strange people have been wandering the grounds.' She looked on with wide eyes at Imogen's meat clever and long filleting knife. They were caked with dried blood. 'Can I see your identity cards, please?'

Jason waved his Glock 19 and patted his slung rifle as he squeezed through the gap. 'These'll have to do for now. We are your only hope of getting to safety.'

The carer gulped as she watched Imogen hop down to reveal a sword strapped to her back. 'Heaven help us!'

Chapter 21

Sitting around the room were ten elderly men and women. Their wide eyes were weary with fatigue. A Zimmer frame was in front of the frailer looking woman and this walking aid was trembling as she grasped it tight in her shaking hands.

'We'll soon get you to safety,' reassured Jason.

All eyes were on his weapons, so he holstered his pistol.

'I've kept us together when things went crazy. I shut the door and we've slept in here as best as we can. In the chairs. There is a toilet outside. I've helped them with their needs. But they haven't eaten since yesterday morning. The chef and his assistant are wedged against the kitchen door. I can't open it,' the carer blurted out in a fast voice. Then she whispered, 'I think they are dead. My mobile won't work. What's going on? My mum will be worried. I should have gone off shift at eight o'clock last night. No one has relieved me.'

Imogen picked up a World War Two gas mask. It was beside a small box with a carrying strap. It smelled old. Its long snout with the green filter at the end reminded her of a womble. The two eye lenses looked sinister. 'Were you all wearing these at the same time yesterday morning?'

One of the men nodded. 'We were doing a reminiscence class. But I told Isabella that these are adult masks. We were issued the child's sizes. We aren't that old,' he said with rising indignation in his voice.

The carer blushed. 'Sorry, William. That was the best I could get from the charity that provides the props for the classes.'

'Don't get upset Isabella, you've done a wonderful job looking after us.' He rose to his feet with the aid of his walking stick. Then, pointing it at Jason and then Imogen, forehead creasing, he asked, 'Are you two vigilantes? Where on earth did you get those pistols and rifles? They look modern military issue.'

Jason shook his head. 'I'm Flight Sergeant Jason Harper. This is Imo.'

'Military. Jolly good. I was a major in the Gordon Highlanders. What's the Royal Air Force doing here? Why isn't the Army deployed?'

'We are tasked with getting you to safety, sir,' replied Jason.

'And how do you propose to do that, young man? Most of us can't walk more than the length of this room. Just what has happened?'

'The Russians attacked this region with chemicals that turned people against each other. The ultimate weapon. Isabella and her masks have saved all your lives,' answered Jason as he looked at each patient, trying to assess their fitness. He pulled out various wrappers from his pouches and handed them around. While the ravenous patients tucked into their food, he turned to Imogen. 'Would you mind going back to the Land Rover and bringing in bottles of water and food for them? They look starved. I think we'd better stay here tonight and find transport in the morning. They can bed down in their own rooms. We'll secure the building when you get back.'

Imogen nodded, reluctantly put down her bladed weapons on the nearest table and jumped through the window again. Sabre sat beneath it, giving out a gentle whine.

'Isabella, can you describe the layout of the building, please? I'll need a route to the manager's office.'

The carer pulled out a pen and notepad and began sketching as she described the best route to the kitchen, the bedrooms, and the office.

The munching and slurping noises grew louder after Imogen returned and handed out goodies. She'd also set up the portable cooker and was boiling a kettle. Grateful eyes were locked onto the supply of tea and the two plastic mugs.

'We'll start with the kitchen, Imogen. Isabella, please take over the tea making and help yourself to the rations. Make sure you have something to eat and drink, too. You've had a long day and night. We'll find you a safe bed once we've secured the building and bedded everyone down for the night.' The small gap in the curtain revealed the darkening evening.

'Will my mum be okay? She's on her own now.'

Jason patted her on her shoulder. 'I'm afraid I don't know. But there is always hope.'

Isabella began crying, and a man rose from his chair and tottered over and put a grandfatherly arm around her and made soothing noises. He nodded at Jason.

'Sabre, stay. Patrol,' ordered Imogen. She hoped the dog understood this command and was pleased to see him sit, alert, between the two ladies. His eyes were ever watchful. One of the ladies reached out and stroked him under the chin.

Jason watched as Imogen picked up her bladed weapons of choice. They seemed appropriate for an attack on the kitchens. Putting his hand on the heavy fire door that had secured the room, he asked, 'Ready?'

She grinned as she held aloft her new toys.

'Okay, I'll open this door, then you go out. We'll go room by room, making our way to the kitchen. We'll take turns going in while the other stands guard outside. Check in wardrobes and the en-suite bathrooms. Even beneath beds. Then check the windows and any patio doors are locked.' He glanced at her tools. 'Don't muck about. Clean kills only.' He pointed his Glock 19 that was in his right hand and pulled open the door with his left and stood aside as she exited the room. He followed straight out.

With a swift check of the unisex toilet immediately outside, they then stormed from bedroom to bedroom, taking just seconds to clear each room. The occupants were in the day lounge, so they weren't expecting any surprises. They soon cleared this wide corridor, big enough for two wheelchairs to pass.

Imogen let out a grunt as she walked into the next bathroom. Jason had pulled the door wide open after she nodded she was ready. The thin-bladed filleting knife was thrust into a snarling woman, unable to work out how to get out of the visitor's toilet. Imogen had caught her, literally, with her pants down. She was now sitting and leaning back on the toilet, her blood spilling over the seat, not quite making it inside the bowl. Imogen didn't bother flushing. 'I'd give that more than five minutes if I were you!'

Jason grimaced as he approached the nursing home's kitchen and waited for her to get into position behind him. It was a push open door, to allow two plates to be carried by the carers. There were lots of black scuff marks about two inches from the ground on the woodwork. He tried to open it with his foot. A gap was permitted, then a blackened hand fell. Jason jumped with fright, ignoring the sniggering coming from Imogen. He shoved with his shoulder and it budged some more. The corpse of the chef, dressed in white and blue chequered jacket and trousers, slide to the floor. His head banged against the door as Jason pushed it further. Two metres away was a similarly dressed woman. Both had blood trails from their jagged throats. Jason picked up the chef and dragged him into the empty dining room. He returned to the assistant and laid her by him, as if they were having a crafty siesta between cooking the dinner. 'We can tell Isabella she can go in and prepare some sort of meal for her patients. They looked half-starved. There are bound to be tinned fruits and biscuits. Maybe even soup she can heat on our stove.' He looked around in the dim light and, looking through the window, could see the sun setting. 'Hey, colonel, how about some power?'

A few seconds later, the lights came on and a cheer erupted from the lounge. Jason put his hand to his mouth at the sight of the thick blood trail he'd caused, which stretched across the floor to the adjacent dining room. It looked like a giant, bleeding slug had made its way between the rooms.

'Let's hope Isabella has a stronger stomach than you.'

Jason winced and pointed at the door to the dining room. 'Let's clear the other rooms. I'll lead.' He was off, leaving Imogen to check the kitchen windows and dining room patio door were locked.

The camera operator had hacked into the nursing home's internal CCTV and was counting the elderly people who were taking it in turns to sip from and pass a steaming mug of tea. The woman with the shaking hands was being helped to drink by Isabella.

The care assistant was gratefully chewing on a protein bar at the same time.

The military camera operator boasted to the colonel, 'There's eleven in the big room.' This was the most that would be rescued from any sector at one time and made her long hours of duty worth it. She sat up straighter in her chair.

Jason gasped as he entered the bedroom. On the bed was a woman, almost skeletal. She'd tussled with her bedding and her nightie was crunched up beyond her thighs. She lay in a pool of her own urine and she'd soiled herself. The faeces had been spread around the bed as she struggled in vain against her attacker. Her mouth was agape, eyes wide and sightless. There was little blood. It looked like whoever had attacked her had drunk well from her torn throat. He ran to the empty en-suite, lifted the toilet seat, and vomited. He allowed the lid to slam shut, perhaps in embarrassment at adding to the smells and excrement in the room.

Imogen stayed silent as she watched from the corridor. As he exited, she shut the door tight.

Scrambling and scratching sounds were coming from the next room. They gave hand signals to each other and prepared themselves for what lay ahead. Jason had his Glock 19 out in the traditional two-handed grip and nodded to her.

The door was pushed open to reveal a male nurse, black trousers, white tunic, crimson with blood, astride a bedbound patient, nuzzling at his neck. The earpieces of a stethoscope were still in his ears, the circular bell piece bounced around their chests. The nurse lifted his head, blood dripping from his feral mouth. Jason put two bullets through his head. Blood, brain, and bone burst from his skull and splattered the knitted bed socks and ragged pyjamas of the long-dead patient. The nurse was thrust backwards from the impact, his spine crunching with the force that propelled him to look like he was limbo dancing. Then he fell from the bed, head taking the brunt of the impact, shattering what remained of his skull. Jason jumped over him and checked the en-suite, projectile vomiting across the shower screen as he walked. He turned, red-faced.

Imogen was patting down the pockets of the nurse. 'I can probably find the medicine cupboard keys. They are bound to have an anti-emetic.' She looked down at the floor. 'It'll be best if you keep the keys. That way, I won't be tempted. There is bound to be potent stuff in there.'

With eyes on the doorway, he replied, 'That's a good idea.' Remembering the shaking hands of the woman, 'Some survivors will need their medicines. Isabella may have enough training and knowledge to help. Pity the qualified nurse succumbed to the chemical attack.' He looked at her chest rig. 'Have you enough until tomorrow?'

She nodded. 'I've got tomorrow's dose of Methadone in my pouch. And another bottle in the Land Rover.'

Jason looked across to the corridor CCTV. 'What a thoughtful colonel we have. How about some personal comms for the next drop off? Then Imogen and I can talk when clearing up your mess.'

Imogen stuck her middle finger up at the camera and gave a toothy grin. 'Communicate this and stick it where the sun doesn't shine!'

Chapter 22

The camera operators all turned to view the one screen. Several left their consoles and walked over to the crowded monitor. Money was discretely changing hands as last-minute bets were placed. A gabble of laughter broke as several hands pointed to Imogen, clear as day, on the screen.

'Enough! Get back to your posts,' screamed the colonel, one hand covering his spasming eye.

The crew returned to their seats, smiling, some still shaking with mirth. It was turning into an entertaining deployment for some.

'There's still one warm body unaccounted for,' barked the colonel.

The screen operator flicked through the CCTV, scanning for a live one.

The duo faced the manager's office, feeling like two summoned workers, about to get the sack or a stern telling off. Only Imogen and Jason were in charge now, and no one could dismiss them. Not when they held such lethal weapons. The door was shut. No noise came from within. The only sound in the building was the distant chatter coming from the dayroom.

Imogen braced herself against the door, hand on the handle. 'After three. One, two,' she pushed down on the handle and thrust open the door, stepping aside for a surprised Jason, 'Three!' she declared in glee.

Jason sprung into the room and quickly scanned it. He took in the desk at the side and the empty large black chair. Three seats and several filing cabinets lined the other side of the room. To the right was a window. It overlooked an enclosed garden, a night light illuminated a small tree, a fountain with still water and some shrubbery. He was checking the locks of the window when he heard a bang on the wood. He didn't bother turning and assumed Imogen was rifling through the desk, looking for new, inventive weapons. Perhaps a sharp letter opener. Then a low growl turned into a breathless pant as something battered against him, forcing his face into the windowpane. His cheek smarted and his teeth bit down on his gums and tongue. There was the sharp, metallic taste of his own blood. He was stuck tight and felt hot breath against his neck. Struggling, he dropped his Glock 19 and tried twisting around, fighting desperately to be free from this tight grip. He was stuck fast against the glass. Hands were scratching furiously against his exposed flesh, tearing down. Fingernails dug deep. He swept his head back in pain. It moved an inch. Then he jerked it back with all his might and got the mother of all headaches as he connected with a forehead. The grip on him relaxed for a moment and he twisted around, pulling out his combat knife. It slid out of its sheath with ease and he stabbed upwards, through a floral blouse and into a well-cupped breast, the figure-improving bra offering no protection against his blade. Jason eased the handle out, ripping more flesh as the barbed edges pulled back. Then he reached higher up and forced the blade through her windpipe, as if performing a tracheostomy, but deeper and wider. There was a retching, gagging noise followed by a gurgling and the manager dropped, her blood-soaked hands giving up the mad scrabble at her own throat as she instinctively tried to stem the flow of blood. As she fell, Jason could now see across the office. Imogen was swinging around in the manager's chair, watching.

Clapping her hands, she offered, in a feigned camp voice, 'I'd give that a seven. The performance was stilted, and it took time for you to find your feet. Your dance partner lacked rhythm, and the tempo was all off. I'd like to have seen more sharp feet movement.'

Jason leaned forward, catching his breath. Drool escaped his lips and dripped onto the carpet. He spat out a clot of blood and cleared his throat, not caring that he'd soiled the thick-piled flooring. Then he stood tall. 'Fuck off, Anton!'

Chuckling, she rifled through the corpse's pocket and withdrew two sets of keys. One looked like they'd open the patio door while the other was for a car. 'I wonder what she drove?'

'I know what I drove. Only my knife through her throat!' declared Jason victoriously.

Imogen nodded approvingly.

Chapter 23

Having secured the building, Jason and Imogen helped Isabella settle the patients into bed. This was a first for the pair, having to undress patients, help them into their night-time continence pads and convince the carer that she was now qualified to dispense their various drugs. Sedation was freely given. Between them, and with the help of the British National Formulary book, they had worked out what the funny spelt words in the patient drug records were for. The patients helpfully told them it was the little white pills they needed.

'Two hours on and off, or four?' asked Jason.

'Eh?' replied Imogen.

'Sleeping while the other stands guard. I'll take first watch. In case we get any of the infected visiting.'

'They'll never get through the toughened glass, will they?'

'I doubt it. But I think Isabella and her charges will settle better knowing one of us is awake.'

Imogen looked along the corridor. They'd convinced the patients to bed down in the rooms on one of the four corridors. Then they'd shut and locked the thick fire doors. She doubted anything could get through them. 'No, I'm wide awake. You get some shuteye.'

Looking sheepish, he remembered what happened to her the last time she went to sleep. 'Okay, thank you. Keep Sabre with you.'

Tickling the dog's ear, she replied, 'Always.'

Walking to their allocated room, he propped open the door with a wooden wedge he found on the floor. He stored his chest rig on the armchair, his rifle on the bedside cabinet, but kept his Glock 19 under the pillow. He slept fully clothed and with his boots on. Sleeping above the covers. He was out within seconds.

Walking to the small kitchen area in the corner of the corridor, Imogen was delighted to find the boiler was chugging away now the electrics had been on for a while. She had instant hot water and made herself a thick black coffee, one in which the teaspoon could almost stand up. She yearned for a flat white instead. She didn't bother checking the small fridge. She knew the milk would be off. She took her drink over to an armchair in the opposite corner, in the small alcove area, popped it on the table and sat down. She leant back and sighed. Closing her eyes, she too soon drifted off to sleep.

The operator silently wished them a good sleep. Her shift was about to end and she knew she'd not sleep as well as Imogen or Jason. She would re-run some of the sights. She had only seen them. How could the duo go to sleep knowing what they had done to their fellow humankind? Working in intelligence, she was sheltered from the muscle fatigue that follows prolonged combat and didn't appreciate that soldiers easily fall asleep after sustained fighting. Their bodies needing to recuperate and restore.

Jason awoke exactly four hours later. His internal alarm clock had been honed after years of operations.

He stretched, slung back on his chest rig, gathered up his weapons and went looking for Imogen.

He found her a few paces away, tucked up in an armchair, coffee cold on the table. Sabre curled up in a ball by the side of the chair. The dog opened one lazy eye and then went back to sleep.

Leaving them both to sleep on, Jason went in search of a coffee and he, too, was delighted that the boiler was working. He even poured water into the sink and had a wash, of sorts. The water soon turned a murky red, then brown, as the day's dirt and blood were washed from his hands and face. Feeling his bristles as he washed, he yearned for a razor and some shaving gel. He made a mental note to go shopping later. He gave up trying to get clean and took his coffee away and stood by the window, peering into the gloom, wondering what Pippa and their unborn child were up to.

A buzzer sounded, causing him to scold himself on hot coffee as he almost dropped his mug. He went striding off to its source.

A light above bedroom three was lit, and he entered. 'How do I turn the noise off?' he hastily asked.

'Sorry, son, force of habit. Hit the glowing button by the side of my bed and put the overhead light on.'

Jason obliged and helped the struggling man to perch on the edge of his bed. He was fumbling inside his pyjama trousers. 'Could you please pass the bed bottle, the plastic one in the bathroom?'

Jason moved quickly. He knew from hearing his grandfather joke how urgent needing a pee in the night could be. As he handed it over, he soon heard a trickle hit the plastic.

'Ah, that's better. I hope I didn't wake you. Damn prostate.'

'No, I was on guard. The others are fast asleep.'

'Thanks, Jason. You've been so busy; I haven't introduced myself.' He gave himself a shake inside the bottle, took out his hand, and thrust it out at Jason. 'I'm Norman. Unlike William, I was a sergeant, like you. We do all the actual work.'

'You're right there Norman. Pleased to meet you.' He shook his hand and made a mental note to wash his hands again. He took the bottle and emptied in down the toilet and placed it on the low cistern.

'My daughter lives in Aberdeen. She's probably dead, isn't she?' sighed Norman. 'Turned into one of those things, or killed by one.'

Jason sensed this old man would probably prefer straight talking. 'I'm afraid so. Unless she was wearing a mask.'

Norman grimaced. 'She was always so particular about her hair and make-up. I doubt she'd have had one on.'

Jason noted he was using past tense and patted him on the hand.

'She was a lovely girl. Just like her mother. She passed eight years ago. I came here about a year ago. Is it rough out there?'

Jason gulped and nodded.

'I served in Palestine. There was always someone ready to shoot you or put a knife in your back. Thank you for what you are doing. I'm ready to get back to sleep. Maybe you should do the same?'

Jason swung Norman's legs back into bed and pulled the covers up. 'Sleep well, Sergeant,' he bid the old man as he switched off the big light.

Chapter 24

The video operator, fresh on her shift, having slept little, watched as Isabella washed and dressed each patient as well as she could, with the aid of Imogen and Jason, carrying water from the only working boiler. Each was sitting with a mug of tea and a packet of biscuits. Bowls of tinned fruit were being prepped in-between nursing duties. Scrambled eggs and porridge were being made in the microwave.

Jason opened the day lounge curtains wide. He wanted to see if any of the infected were roaming. He tasked William and Norman to keep a watch from their comfy leather armchairs.

Imogen was slowly feeding the lady with the constantly shaking hand. Between mouthfuls of tea and shortbread, she had introduced herself as Jean and thanked Imogen for her patience. 'My friend isn't here. Is this all of us who survived?' She looked gloomily around the dayroom.

'I'm so sorry, we couldn't save anymore. We were too late. We didn't know you were here until last night.'

Tears formed in Jean's eyes and Imogen plucked a tissue from a box on the table and dabbed at them.

'She had dementia. It's probably for the best. She didn't know me. Not for the last few months. It's like her ability to move faded with her memory. She was bedbound. In the room next to me.'

Imogen thought to the room they'd locked behind them, to stop patients going in and seeing the awful sight. This was as cruel as the swimming pool scenes. Her reverie was soon broken by a young hand, who took a turn in lifting the mug to Jean's lips.

'I'll take over. You get your breakfast, Imogen,' suggested Isabella. 'Could I then pop home and check on my mother? We only live three streets away.'

Imogen firmly shook her head. 'Only if you want to get yourself killed.'

Isabella opened her mouth to argue, then gave a gasp as one of the infected took a run at the patio door, went headfirst into the toughened glass, and appeared to rebound. He lay prone on the patio flagstones for a few seconds, then went wandering off. She stuttered, 'I'll just stay here, then.'

'That'll be best,' heeded Imogen as she wandered over to the table with the rations she'd taken from the Land Rover last night and began cooking some bacon grill. Seeing William's and Norman's eyes light up, she opened several more cans and got them ready to throw in the pan once these had cooked. She had a feeling she'd be eating a late breakfast.

Isabella wandered over, and they were joined by Jason, who had been helping a frail woman to sit down. 'How will you get us to safety?' asked the young carer. 'Do we meet in the Town Hall? With other survivors?' She thought of her mum.

'No. We must get you out of Aberdeenshire. There is a special meeting point. A good twenty miles away,' replied Imogen, hoping she got the distance right. 'Do you have a minibus?'

'No. Even if we did, half of the patients won't be able to climb the few stairs. Some will need to go in wheelchairs. The rest need transport they can simply step into. We haven't anything like that. Will we have to stay here?'

'That's not an option,' said Jason as he watched two of the infected trade punches on the patio. The fight ended after one landed a hefty kick into the groin of the other. Jason winced in sympathy.

'Don't worry,' laughed Imogen. 'I have an idea.'

Chapter 25

Jason crouched outside on the patio and shot at several of the infected crowded around a raised flower bed. They dropped dead, torsos landing on the varnished railway sleepers, heads on the earth, flattening flowers as Imogen ran out with Sabre. She reached the Land Rover, opened the door, pointed for Sabre to get in, and pushed him over to the passenger seat as she squirmed in. She gunned the engine and zoomed off, running down an elderly man walking about in mud-encrusted pyjamas and a half-opened silk dressing-gown. His eyes glowed red as his face disappeared under the wheels of the vehicle. Imogen gave out a cackle as she heard his skull crack under the force of the wheels. The Land Rover rocked from side to side and then trundled off.

Jason waiting a few more minutes, scanning the area for danger, then returned to the dayroom. He carefully locked the patio door and did what every military person traditionally did between parts of a mission — he made a brew for everyone.

'Where the fuck is she going in such a hurry?' questioned the colonel aloud.

The operator stayed silent.

'Well, don't just sit there, follow that car.'

Several of the operators smirked at the choice of phrase. One wondered if the colonel thought he was in a ham spy movie from the fifties. He didn't dare say this aloud, though.

The young operator furiously clicked away at her mouse and keyboard, trying to keep up with Imogen's fast driving.

Imogen skidded to a halt outside the mini grocery shop by the town square. She leapt out and grabbed the bag she had filled yesterday. Sabre licked his lips as he caught a scent of what was thrown into the back of the Land Rover.

A woman came running out of the shop, wearing a tabard with the shop's logo on it. She made for Imogen, as if protesting at the theft of her products.

Imogen clocked her blood-encrusted chin and reached for her sword. 'Damn!' She cursed herself for taking off the harness and letting the sword drop to the floor, along with her bladed weapons, when she curled up in the armchair in the early hours. As the woman reached her, Imogen punched her full in the face, hearing bone shatter. Then she side kicked at her, contacting harshly with her ankles, forcing the infected woman off her feet. She landed with a sickening thud as her skull shattered on the harsh pavement. Taking no time to look, she whipped out her trusty catapult and dwindling supply of ball bearings and began shooting them into the crowd rushing at her from the adjacent bank. She deposited the speeding armaments into their foreheads, jaws, and throats, dropping the eight-strong group. With a final twang, she stuffed her weapons back into her combat trousers' side pocket and shot off in the Land Rover.

'I want her on my team when I next deploy,' chuckled the colonel to no one in particular.

The sergeant who was running the side bets wondered if the colonel wanted to lay a wager on the number of kills the feral woman could accumulate. Then thought better of it. His hustle was proving a nice little earner and he didn't want any officer to spoil it for him.

The Land Rover screeched to a halt after crossing the bridge, the wheels skidding in some blood patches. Four women wearing white tunics and black trousers were standing on the road, waving their hands in the air. One shouted, 'Stop.'

Imogen was intent on driving through them, but had never heard the infected speak. She knew they were fellow survivors. Her feet hesitated on the accelerator. 'For fuck's sake,' she muttered as she hit the brakes and the Land Rover came to a juddering halt inches from the group.

Putting the vehicle into gear and pulling the handbrake, she commanded Sabre, 'Out, boy.' She pulled open her door, jumped out, clucking her tongue for him to follow. 'The fuck you lot want?'

The oldest of the quartet, a paper mask tucked under her chin, like a hammock, replied in a shaky voice, 'What's going on? We saw you earlier. With the man, shooting. We've been too scared to come out.' She pointed to a nearby nail bar, the door open. The saloon was empty of infected corpses. 'We locked the door when the rioting started. We hid in the basement stockroom.' Her eyes went wide. 'People started killing each other,' she confided to Imogen.

'No shit, Sherlock!'

Another of the women, about nineteen and with the same amount of smudged make-up as the others, looked up at Imogen with tear-stained mascara. 'Please, help us.'

'All right. Shut the fuck up. Stop bleating.' Imogen stared at the two younger women who were cuddling together for comfort, crying. They stopped. Imogen rolled her eyes and stifled a yawn. 'There's been a Russian assault by plane with chemicals. Now it's a zombie attack. Stonehaven has been turned into a zombie haven. Careful you don't get killed,' she heeded in a chilling voice.

The four shivered and moved closer together, their eyes darting around them. One risked, 'For real?'

'Yep. Just like in the movies.' Imogen lifted her rifle. 'I'm here to clean up this town.' She wished her cowboy was here to listen to that one-liner. She beamed, proud of her new job.

'Do you have weapons for us?' one of the nail technicians offered?

'Piss off, I wouldn't trust you lot with a gun. You aren't trained. I am. Were you all wearing paper masks?'

'Yes, to protect us from the dust and chemicals we use. It's easier to keep them on all day. We'd just opened yesterday when it kicked off.'

'They saved your lives. Be thankful. Now bugger off out of it and don't get in my way. I've something important to do. Find a car. Not this one. If you see it parked, don't nick it. Or I'll find you.' She lifted her rifle menacingly.

The foursome took a step back, like a small squad of guardsmen on parade. 'Will you come with us, and guard us while we find one?'

Imogen smirked, 'Fuck off. I'm not babysitting you.' She knew Jason wouldn't approve, but she didn't care. He wasn't here to ruin her fun. She let off a round at their feet and the bullet thudded into the concrete, centimetres from the youngest. She cackled as they jumped, screamed, and ran back to the safety of their nail bar. She shouted at their backs, 'Now fuck off out of it and don't get in my way. Head south, towards Dundee. Stop in the ditch with the great articulated lorry sticking out.' She puffed out her chest and stood tall. 'That was me! If you see a smug colonel, tell him Imogen says hello, and he's a cocksucker!'

'Get me the fucking drone operator on comms,' bayed the colonel. 'How on earth did he miss those four? Who else has he missed?' The officer paced the room, his fists clenching and unclenching. 'Put him on speaker. I want you all to hear me rip his fucking head off.' Pointing at the sergeant, 'Find me another drone. I want a fresh sweep of the area. I need more survivors.' His eye began its regular twitch. 'I can't go to my brigadier with only a handful. He'll never deploy me in a hotspot again,' he whispered as he rubbed feverishly at his eye.

The sergeant smirked as he heard what Imogen said to the nail technicians. The colonel had been too busy muttering to himself again to hear over their hacked CCTV.

The reinforced glass didn't shatter as Imogen's SA80 stock thudded on it. She cursed as it bounced fruitlessly off. 'I really want that watch,' she told Sabre, sat attentively a foot away. She looked around the jeweller's shop for a suitable piece of rubble to throw at the window. 'Just my luck to stop outside a building that hasn't been damaged.' She gave up looking for a brick and took a step back, reassessing her situation. She pointed her rifle at the window, about to let off a few rounds, when bolts from the door were pulled back. She heard a key turn, and the door opened a fraction. A can of pepper spray was thrust out and squirted ineffectually into the air around her chest. Imogen punched down on the wrist with all her might and the can was dropped and rolled away. A gruff man's voice yelled out in pain as Imogen caused further injury to him by thrusting open the door and barging in. Wood and toughened glass banged into him, forcing him to the ground.

Imogen walked casually in, as if a shopper browsing with no intent to rush a purchase. 'Morning fella, that's you open now, is it?' She stared at him, waiting for his pain-ridden eyes to open, rifle at the ready.

'Don't shoot!' he screamed.

'Not infected then?'

'Infected? Is that why everyone is trying to rob and kill me? Would a disease work that quickly?'

'Yeah. But you've got yourself a nice little fortress here. Nothing can get in. How did you escape the fumes?'

'Fumes? Is that how the disease spread? I doubt I'd have seen them, anyway. I was cleaning an antique watch. I wear gloves and a mask so as not to introduce any dirt in the workings. I couldn't finish it. The power went off. Then the water. I'm so hungry and thirsty. I don't keep food here.'

'Not such a strong fortress, then. You need to leave now and make for Dundee. You'll find a military checkpoint there and will get processed.'

He shook his head briskly. 'I'm not leaving my stock. My shop will get robbed. I thought that was what you were doing.'

Withdrawing her combat knife slowly, relishing the sound it made coming out of its sheath, she watched gleefully as he gulped and his eyes went wide. 'I'm under orders to kill any survivors, infected, or perhaps otherwise. Who's to know?'

Pointing at the cameras above his display cases and till, he stuttered, 'You'll be filmed. You can't do this.'

Talking a step towards him, she grinned. 'Power's off, dickhead.'

Grabbing his car keys, he ran past her and out onto the street.

Sabre gave a few wags of his tail, hoping to give chase.

Imogen shook her head. 'Stay here with me. We've some shopping to do, lad.'

The colonel's mouth was open as he stared at the screen. 'She wouldn't dare,' he muttered after a few seconds of watching her re-sheathing her knife and picking up some carrier bags by the till. He watched as she took a heavy-duty fire extinguisher to the display cabinets and cracked them open as easily as a teaspoon to a boiled egg's top. She filled the bags up with watches and rings from the shop, making several trips to the Land Rover. 'Open up a new frame and track that man. Make sure he gets to the processing area. Alert them to his arrival and tell them to get a full statement about her actions. Make sure all this is recorded.'

A jolly toot of a horn alerted Jason to the approaching vehicle. Norman and William were grinning from ear to ear. Jason opened the patio door and walked around to the car park. 'What the actual fuck!' he yelled as he saw what she was busy reversing to where he'd parked the Land Rover the evening before.

She killed the engine and jumped out; a bloodstained train driver's hat with crumpled peak was perched cheekily on her head to one side. Sabre jumped out of one of the Land Train's carriages. 'All right, Cowboy!' she greeted him as she reached into a carriage, pulled out a wedge of wood, and placed a wooden ramp by the rim of the entrance to the carriage.

'A wheelchair will go straight up to that. No messing about,' he laughed with glee.

She curtseyed, 'You're welcome!'

'Clever, so clever! Well done, Imo!'

She beamed. 'I'll drive. It took me a while to work out the controls. I've left some goodies from the Land Rover in the back carriage for you to keep busy with if we encounter any of the infected.' She reached for her pistol. 'I'll give this to Norman. I bet he knows how to handle it. He can sit in the middle. Give yours to the major. Then we've a defence, of sorts. This doesn't go fast, so things could get hairy. Those infected can run fast and the carriages are open.'

He nodded as he peered into his carriage. There was The Long and the box of grenades, as well as fresh ammunition for his SA80. He lifted a fresh box of bullets for the Glock 19. It was time to give the major and sergeant a quick firearms lesson while Isabella helped the others onto the Land Train.

Applause and whoops filled the Ops Room and a few of the braver operators left their post and slapped backs and high-fived their friends.

The colonel gave a quick smile and then became his usual stony-faced self as he snarled, 'What do you think this is, Hollywood? Get back to your posts and concentrating on your sectors.' In a quiet voice, only heard by the operator monitoring Imogen, he whispered, 'Resourceful. What a resourceful soldier she is. She'd make a great Special Forces operative.'

'We can stop off by the Land Rover and you can drive behind us, if you like,' suggested Imogen. 'All our gear is in it and the vehicle is indestructible. It'll be a shame to lose it. Talking of which, I'm not leaving our cooker behind. I'd hate not to get our fried bacon roll in the mornings. Or a brew.'

As she went wondering off, Jason knew she thought they wouldn't get through the fence when they escorted the pensioners and carer to the colonel. Otherwise, she'd leave the gadget here. His heart sank. Would he ever get through the fence?

A voice broke into his thoughts. 'Jean has her wheelchair brakes applied and I've sat the others on cushions in the carriages. They should be comfortable.'

'Thanks Isabella, you're doing great.' He went around the Land Train, checking each passenger. He stopped at Jean's carriage. Her head was shaking and her eyes were darting around. Jason took her hand and then placed his other on top of it to stop her shaking. It didn't work. 'Maybe it'll be best to close your eyes, Jean. When we get going. Then open them when we come to a stop.'

She looked him in the eyes, and a brief smile passed her lips. 'I was eight when the blitz started down in London. I saw some sights, before I was evacuated to the country. I survived the war. Nothing fazes me.'

'That can't have been an easy time. We'll keep you safe.'

'I know. You make a great team, you, and Imo. You remind me of my late husband. That's why I moved up to Stonehaven. We met in London. He was doing his National Service. We took over his family's farm. The outdoor life suited me. Whenever the sights revisited me, I'd get out into the fields to find calm. Promise me, when this nightmare is over, you'll get Imo into a field. Help her find her inner calm. Both of you. The things you are doing for your country are more than anyone can be expected to cope with. Bless you for saving us.' Tears fell from her eyes and she removed her hand from his grip and wiped them away as best as she could.

Jason nodded, not trusting his voice for several seconds. 'I will,' he murmured. 'She deserves that.' He thought back to Tex's assault. 'After all she's gone through.'

'You both do,' affirmed Jean.

Jason looked down at the wheelchair brakes, double-checking Isabella had secured this precious woman. He patted her on the hand and moved on to the next carriage.

Imogen slotted a fresh magazine into her SA80 and placed it on her lap. She patted her catapult pocket, checking her favourite weapon was still there and then turned on the ignition. She turned around, smiled at Sabre, whose tongue was lolling out to the side. He was sat on the seat immediately behind her.

Jason nodded to Norman. 'You good?'

The former sergeant gave a quick nod back. 'It's been a long time, but I know I'll come good. This fancy pistol of yours is so much lighter than the one I fired so many years ago. I'll just point and shoot at anyone who gets close enough.'

Jason patted his SA80. 'It's a backup plan. This and my sniper rifle should stop any of the infected in their tracks.'

A long toot of the Land Train whistle broke into their conversation. It was followed by three short blasts. A pair of collared doves in the nearby tree flew off in protest at the noise.

'Time to mount up, soldier!' exclaimed Norman, his eyes alight with fresh fervour.

Jason grinned. He knew the old sergeant and major would defend the other passengers until their dying breath. He hoped it wouldn't come to that.

Chapter 26

Imogen weaved the Land Train around the piles of corpses they'd made in Stonehaven. She took each turn in an exaggerated arc to allow the carriages to bend and curve like a snake. She'd planned the route and had spent valuable time this morning leaping off the Land Rover and dragging some bodies to the pavement. Her acts were not entirely selfless. She had stripped the corpses of more jewellery and left her booty in the back of the Land Rover. She knew Jason wouldn't mind.

Jean gasped at the cairn-like pile of bodies by the doorway of the local fish and chip takeaway, the favourite of the nursing home. Limbs were entwined around others like a macabre game of human Jenga. Strangers in life had become friends in death. She looked away, yearning for her simple life as a sheep farmer.

The Land Train's engine protested as they turned at the former police station and twisted up the hill by the pretty church with the proud gardens. Flower beds now boasted corpses of parishioners who would not grow anymore. The locomotive steadily climbed the steep rise and Norman whistled sharply through his teeth as he saw the devastation of the petrol station and the blackened corpses that had finally burnt out. His fingers on the pistol turned white in his steadfast grip.

Other former residents of the nursing home cried out and allowed tears to flow as they saw the destruction of their cherished town and the number of bodies of what could have been friends and family that littered the streets. Several closed their eyes tight.

Imogen did not have the heart to blow the train whistle again. She sensed the sombre mood of her passengers.

A sharp crack echoed around the old Victorian houses and a running woman, carrying the head of a toddler, fell to the ground. The head rolled down the hill, making its way under the wheels of the Land Train, and then was squashed, like a small pumpkin dropped from a height. A squelch broke the silence and the carriage it was under listed to the side and then corrected itself. Its passenger, William, gave the sign of the cross with his free hand. The other had been aiming at the woman and he gave a brief prayer for both their lives and thanked his God that he hadn't needed to pull the trigger.

Imogen coaxed more speed from the Land Train and its precious cargo. A steely grimace was set in her face. She was determined to save these brave pensioners. She spotted a teenager come running out of the trees ahead of them. He arced around and made straight for her. She pulled up her SA80, resting it on the steering wheel, judging her aim as best as she could, and sprayed him with bullets.

His torso juddered as rounds blasted into him, almost cutting him in half. His arms splayed out, doing nothing to prevent his fall. Imogen simply altered her course and drove around him as he took a last gasping breath through his blood-encrusted mouth. She pulled up alongside their trusty, battered old Land Rover. It looked dull compared to the garishly painted Land Train and carriages. She turned off the engine, allowing the overworked parts to rest.

Whistling for Sabre to dismount, she shouted across, 'Patrol!'

Sabre leapt down from his seat. Tongue back in his mouth, having cooled down thanks to the breeze coming through his open-air carriage during the drive. He had enjoyed sticking his head out of the passenger window whenever his former owner took him for a drive. A dormant memory made him go sniffing for him as he patrolled around the two vehicles and carriages.

William rose from his seat and tottered over to the Land Rover, one hand on his pistol, the other leaning into his walking stick. Jason and Imogen joined him. 'Sorry about the bumps,' confessed Imogen.

'You are doing well, Imogen,' replied William, a brisk tone in his voice. He turned to Jason, 'As are you, young man. Your sniper skills are needed to get us safely to this fence you've described.'

'He's got a badge for it,' proudly boasted Imogen.

Jason patted his sleeve. 'It's on my other uniform.'

The old major chuckled. 'My troops were always trying to earn one. They were after the extra pay. And the kudos, of course. They measured everything in the number of pints. They knew it would be enough for another drink at the NAAFI each evening.'

Jason grinned. 'Nothing has changed. Though the price of a pint is probably astronomical from your day.'

William looked around and then behind them, at the trail of destruction they'd left. The silence was eerie, especially being this close to the once bustling A90. 'Let me drive the Land Rover. You need to defend the troops against attacks. Those who are infected look lethal.' He looked down at his walking stick. 'I'm not sure I could be as brave as the pair of you and kill the infected. Even though I know it's the right thing to do. It really did surprise me when you said there is no cure.'

'That's no problem, Major. You've done your service.' Jason looked across to the Land Rover and back to William. 'Do you know how to drive one of these?'

Chuckling, William replied, 'Probably long before you pair were even a glint in your father's eyes. The

Land Rover was the military workhorse, and I used to get my driver to sit in the passenger seat. That's probably why I was never promoted to colonel. I liked getting involved, not simply dishing out the orders.'

Imogen's hand tightened around her rifle grip at the mention of the word colonel. She looked longingly ahead of her. 'Okay, that's settled. You take the rear and when I stop, pull up alongside us so that Jason has a full arc of fire. I suspect we'll have a clear route to the fence.' She thought back to their previous journey in the JCB and then in the articulated truck. She smirked at the memory.

'Brilliant!' declared William. 'It'll just be like old times.' His face reddened. 'There's just one problem.'

Jason frowned.

Sheepishly, William blurted out, 'You'll have to help this old soldier up in his seat. The old hips and knees won't make it there on their own.'

Chapter 27

The screen operator followed the strange procession along the A90 as they made their way south at a steady twenty miles an hour. They had a straight and clear road, the JCB and truck had seen to that. She watched as Jason sighted down his sniper rifle and squeezed the trigger. Somewhere in the distance, a former farm worker fell, his belly full from feeding on cattle. She patched into the next CCTV, hidden in a lamppost, to reveal Jason leaning over the carriage side and vomiting. The crystal-clear image showed the orange-green liquid being caught in the wind and spraying onto the Land Rover's windscreen. This vehicle's indicators briefly flashed as the old major tried to find the screen wash and wiper blade switch.

'What assets in the air do we have?' barked the colonel.

The sergeant to the left of him shouted across, 'Nothing, sir. All helicopters and armed drones are all deployed in the other sectors. The resistance is heavy in those areas.' He'd had to work furiously at keeping his numbers correct for the book he was running for the unit. Sector four had the most kills, though Imogen's sector was the most imaginative and entertaining. He wished he'd been allocated that screen.

The colonel's hand shot up to his left eye and laid it flat, as if having an eye test at an optician. He didn't see any better when he removed it to wipe at imaginary sweat from his brow. 'Damn,' he muttered.

Jason moved to the other side of the carriage. A flash of yellow had caught his eye. He stared down through his scope and an angry face, deep red eyes, came into sharp focus. It was carrying a litter picker long handled grabber tool. A still baby was hooked on the end. Jason steadied his breathing at the shocking sight and took no pleasure in pulling the trigger. He didn't watch as the man fell, dead. He was certain of the kill.

A rattle of firepower broke his reverie, and he watched as a man, dressed in a breakdown uniform, fell in a hail of bullets from Imogen's rifle. No member of the fourth emergency services would be coming to his rescue. The carriages weaved slightly at the lapse in concentration at Imogen's driving and her foot came off the accelerator. Then she regained control of the Land Train and they accelerated to their destination.

After a few miles, the Land Train screeched to a halt. Jason assumed they'd reached the pile of corpses the helicopter the day before had gunned down. He didn't relish the prospect of moving them out of the way. He jumped out of the carriage and ran towards the front. A surprised look crossed his face. 'Where are all the corpses?' His nose wrinkled as a waft of lingering sweetness passed by. He stared into the distant hill and saw the rising plumes of smoke. 'Burning flesh.'

Imogen glanced at where he was gazing with his faraway, haunted look. 'How do you know?'

'Once you've smelt it, you'll never forget it. The military worry about the spread of diseases like cholera and typhoid. They must have cleared up the road of the corpses and are now mass burning them in a big pit. I bet they used a reinforced-glass bulldozer and some sort of dumper truck to scoop them up and ensure the safety of the drivers. They probably had a squad of my old regiment to guard them. Maybe even that helicopter we kept seeing in Aberdeen.' He shivered at the thought of what that sight would have looked like. 'Pity they won't use their precious personnel to do the killing instead of us.' He thought back to Tex and wondered how quickly they'd clear Stonehaven. He was glad they'd not left much evidence of that crime.

Imogen placed a hand gently on his shoulder and then gripped it. 'Not our problem, remember?'

Jean shot her arm out from her carriage, almost tipping herself from her wheelchair, interrupting the couple. 'Look, you two. Someone is alive in that car in the layby. I can see tiny arms moving about.'

The duo broke off their clasp and ran forward the few metres. Jason pointed to the left and Imogen rounded the far side while he went to the driver's side. Through the window, he could see a woman slumped over the steering wheel. Dried blood encrusted over her purple face. He surmised that she must have braked sharply from the main road and hit her head. The car had come to a halt in front of a fixed to the ground heavy-duty rubbish bin. Its bolts on the tarmac hadn't prevented it from tilting with the impact.

Imogen glanced in the empty front seat, then took a step backwards and her eyes widened. 'He's alive. We've saved a child. Thank God.' She tried the door and was relieved to find it unlocked. She'd had enough of glass not yielding to her touch today. Opening the door wide, she made soothing noises to the crying boy and spoke softly. 'It's all right, son. We'll soon get you out.' As she released the buckles, she gently scooped him in her arms and whispered, 'Come with Auntie Imo. Do you like dogs? Sabre is going to love you. He's a big softy.' She shielded his eyes from the sight of his dead mother and led him away. 'Look at our choo-choo. Do you like trains?'

The boy's tears dried up, and a grin stretched across his face at the sight of the giant Land Train. 'I want to be a train driver when I grow up.'

Imogen smiled down at him. 'That's a great job to have. Would you like to drive with me? I'll let you blow the whistle.'

He tried to wriggle out from her embrace. 'Will mum come with us? She loves trains too.'

'No dear. She's having a sleep. Let's leave her to rest.' She watched out of the corner of her eye as Jason unfurled a blanket from the boot of the car and draped it over the boy's mother so the boy wouldn't see her face as they drove past in the Land Train. 'She won't mind if you have an adventure with me and my dog, Sabre.'

The screen operator dabbed at her eyes with a piece of tissue paper and ignored the sighing of the colonel behind her as he muttered, 'Thank Christ, they've found a child.'

Imogen drove at a slower rate, not wanting to scare the young boy. Her eyes were constantly scanning head and to their left and right. She was bringing all her cargo safely to the colonel, especially the boy. 'What's your name?'

'Liam. I'm four,' he innocently offered.

'Do you see that big switch there, Liam?'

'Yes, the blue one?'

'That's right. Lean forward and press it down.'

Liam did as his new Auntie Imo asked. He gave a joyful giggle as the train's horn thundered into the sky. He tooted it several times in a row, making a tune he liked.

Jason scanned the area for the undead, then, looking ahead and over the carriage's roofs, he saw a watchtower, about a kilometre away. As they neared, he could make out the large shape of a General-Purpose Machine Gun. Two heads bobbed about. Both wore helmets. He sighed. 'I'll get to you, Pippa. Somehow,' he promised. Looking away, he glanced at William, faithfully following the strange transport. Jason marvelled at this generation. Each of the nursing home residents had lived through the tough Second World War years. Had grown up and thrived. Then some had fought their own wars in Aden and

Palestine, maybe even Korea. And yet they remained uncomplaining, steadfast in their adversity. It was Isabella who seemed the most nervous, jumping around her carriage every few seconds. Leaping in the air with each bullet crack. She had screamed several times during the journey, alerting Jason to another inbound, infected person. He didn't know it, but the sergeant running bets at the Ops Room did: Jason was about to surpass Imogen's kill rate. He watched on, through his scope, as the fence loomed nearer.

Imogen took her foot off the accelerator and eased it onto the brake of this automatic vehicle. It had taken her a few minutes to work out, earlier in the morning, how to drive this tourist-enticing vehicle. It had been odd not having to worry about gears. Her left foot felt idle as she only needed to use her right to pump the accelerator or brake.

'Well, you've been busy,' she muttered as she approached a long concrete barrier that stretched across the A90. No vehicle was getting through that. A three-foot gap was built into the side and then another barrier stretched across towards the embankment. She halted, turned off the ignition and, turning around to face her charges, yelled, 'We are on foot from here. It's a brief walk to the fence. Then you are safe.' Grabbing her rifle and then taking Liam by his small hand, she went to the carriage where Isabella was helping a lady get to her feet. 'Escort her through the gap. I'll take Jean.' She released Liam's hand, squatted by him, gave him a tight cuddle, and took his hand and placed it in Isabella's free hand. She brushed aside his loose hair from his fringe. 'You go with your Auntie Isabella now, Liam. Be brave.'

The boy looked up at this new relative and narrowed his eyes in confusion. He was looking around him, seeing if his mum was here. Tears were forming in his eyes.

'It's all right, you'll be safe now. Off you go,' encouraged Imogen, fighting back tears. She swallowed several times.

Isabella, eyes wide, looking constantly around her, nodded, and taking the boy to the next carriage, she reached for the woman's hand, guided her off the carriage and kept hold of her and Liam until they disappeared through the gap.

Placing the wooden ramp by the carriage, Imogen gleefully told Jean, 'We'll soon have you off and through to safety. Well done for spotting Liam, the boy. We've done something good, something great, today.' She looked up, surprised that Jean's hands were no longer shaking. She looked up to her still head, slunk to her chin, and a surprised, 'Oh,' escaped her lips. 'You poor cow. A life for a life. What a fucking cruel world it is.' Imogen stretched across and closed Jean's eyes. Turning swiftly, she lifted the wooden ramp and went to the next carriage, tentatively at first, relieved to hear this woman talk to her. She put down the ramp and offered her arm in aid. This pair headed off, one shuffling, the other wanting desperately to break into a stride, through the gap in the long, concrete bollards.

Chapter 28

'How nice to meet you again, Imo,' smirked the colonel, a cigar clenched in his teeth.

'Fuck off, dickhead. Here are the survivors. A town that big probably killed each other on day one of the attack. Too many infected, I'd guess. We did our best.' She made to move past him, towards the gateway that Isabella and her charges had gone through. She had watched as a soldier, in what looked like full riot gear, heavily padded from top to toe, came up to them and checked their eyes with some sort of scanner. He looked like the Michelin man wearing an American footballer's helmet and face visor.

'Stay the fuck where you are,' ordered the colonel as he talked into a phone.

A padded-up soldier took the old woman's arm and pointed across to Imogen for the benefit of Isabella. The young care assistant walked back, smiled at Imogen, and took the hand of her other patient. 'Thank you for getting us to safety, Imo.'

Imogen nodded; rifle slung low in her hand. She looked back at the colonel. 'Jason needs to get through that. To see his wife.'

'Not happening. You are too much of an asset. You make a mighty fine killing machine. I'd have been proud to have fought alongside you in the regiment.'

'What regiment?' she asked, frowning.

Jason sidled up, 'He means the Special Air Service.' He took the pistols from William and Norman and was shaking their hands.

'Cool! Do I get a special badge and beret?'

The two old men saluted to Jason, and he returned their salute after holstering his weapon. He watched as they turned and shuffled off through the first part of the fence. A small hut had been built into the section of no-man's-land. It formed a guardroom of sorts. Jason handed Imogen back her Glock 19. 'I doubt it.' He turned to face the colonel. 'You're not letting us through, are you?'

Grinning, the colonel took his time in nodding, taking satisfaction in seeing the drooping shoulders of Jason and the look of sheer fatigue and anguish cross his face. 'We don't have the resources. Our troops are being deployed. They are on a war footing.'

Jason swallowed hard, his mouth drying. 'That's going to be bloody.'

'Not your problem, soldier.' He pressed some buttons on his phone and Jason's pocket beeped. 'A fresh grid reference.' He looked on as the last of the patients were helped by Isabella. 'I guess you did well.'

Jason threw down his SA80. It clattered on the road's surface. 'I refuse. I'm done.'

The colonel grinned. 'Three went in, only two came out.'

'Eh?' interrupted Imogen.

'To the room in Stonehaven. It looked like quite the party,' beamed the colonel.

'Why, you-' snarled Imogen as she withdrew her combat knife and lunged at the colonel.

The officer quickly sidestepped and brought down his hand in a clean chop just above her wrist, temporarily numbing her hand. The blade dropped.

Imogen let out a gasp and cradled her unfeeling hand in her other. 'Bastard!'

Sabre growled, his hackles up. Jason hissed for him to stay.

'It's terrible, the war crimes we witness. Then there is the looting. We always prosecute, eventually.' The colonel looked up at the sky. 'We've cameras everywhere.'

'Don't say a word, Imo,' heeded Jason.

'That's too late a warning, soldier. We record everything.'

'What do you want?' replied Jason, reluctantly picking up his rifle.

'That's my boy.' The colonel pointed to two kitbags placed by the concrete barriers. 'You'll find fresh supplies, as requested. Everything you need for your next op. Speaking of operations, you don't remember me, do you?'

Jason eyed the colonel. 'No, sir.'

'Oh yes you do, sunshine. Remember Yemen.'

Jason rubbed his jaw. 'I'm not likely to forget Yemen.'

'Nor will I,' shouted the colonel, spittle flying from his mouth, his free hand clenching. He took two deep breaths, composing himself. Calmly, he continued, 'Like your old friend there, I was a major when you knew me.'

'You're able to hear our conversations? Otherwise, how would you know the old boy was a major?'

The colonel nodded smugly.

Light dawned on Jason's face, and a grave look chiselled its way onto his face. 'I'm sorry. I've more than made up for it since, Major Winters.'

'Colonel Winters. I've fought on, done my duty, earned my rank. Honoured those who died.' He stabbed a finger into Jason's shoulder repeatedly. 'Because of you and your reluctance to kill a terrorist.'

Jason looked up defiantly, taking the blows to his shoulder. 'We should have had better intelligence. To prepare us.'

'No amount of planning survives the first battle, you know that.'

Jason looked down at his boots. 'I do now.' He looked back at the colonel, pleadingly, 'Please let me see my wife.'

'The wife and girlfriends of Paul Bradley, Barry Mackenzie, and Ash Miller didn't get to see their loved ones alive again, thanks to you.'

Jason looked down at his boots at the mention of the three names that were etched into his heart. They were never far from his thoughts. He looked up and jutted out his chin. 'We've done what you asked. We cleared the infected in Stonehaven and rescued survivors.'

'It doesn't redeem you. They were the finest of soldiers.'

Jason fell to his knees, his rifle falling from his grasp. 'I can't go on. It's terrible what we've done.'

The colonel looked from him to Imogen. 'Yes, mighty terrible. Poor Tex. Or was his name Bob? Get on your feet, soldier.'

Imogen reached down, whispered, 'Don't let the bastard see you like this,' and helped him back up. She then handed him back his rifle.

'And what about you, Imo? What would you like?'

She thought about it for a second as she watched the last of the nursing home patients walk through to the second gateway and disappear through the second fence. It felt good to have helped others. To have saved so many lives. Especially young Liam. 'I've nowhere I need to be.'

'You've no one, have you? From a broken home, a shattered family.'

She looked at Jason. 'I've friends. That's deeper than family. I get to choose who I love now.'

'That's so sweet,' murmured the colonel, sarcasm heavily laden in his voice. He took a long draw from his cigar, blew out several smoke rings, and idly watched them drift off. Then he pressed a few buttons on his phone screen. The mobile in Jason's pocket rang.

Chapter 29

The colonel walked away, waving in the air as he strode off. 'Don't keep her waiting,'

Imogen and Jason glanced at each other, then Jason fumbled in his pocket. He looked on in disbelief as the screen merely said Pippa. He quickly slung his rifle and pressed to accept the call. 'Is it really you?' he croaked out.

Juddering breathing filled the air and then Pippa replied, 'Yes, my darling, it's me. Where are you?'

Jason held the phone nearer to his ear, wishing he could bring her to him. 'On the border with Angus, on the A90. They've built a big fence around Aberdeenshire. The military.'

'What! There has been a news embargo. Things went crazy at the hospital. Ian tried to kill me. He was shot by a marksman in a helicopter, then it landed and whisked us away to a processing building in Dundee. We had lots of medical tests. I got released this morning. I'm staying with my mum and dad.'

Jason let out a sigh. 'Thank God. Is our baby safe?'

'Yes, my love, he's kicking away. What's happening?'

Tears fell from Jason and he used the back of his combat gloves to wipe them away. 'It was a chemical attack. By the Russians. People who came into contact with it started killing each other. They still are.'

'Christ!' exclaimed Pippa. 'Are you okay?'

Jason sighed. 'They made the ultimate weapon and tested it on the people of Aberdeen and the shire. I can't get through the fence. I've been called up to the Reserve. I'm back in my old role as a sniper and gunner.'

'But you've left that life. You're about to retrain as a carpenter.'

'Legally, there is nothing I can do.'

'What are the military expecting you to do?'

More tears fell. 'I've had to kill again, Pippa. There is no cure. I must kill the infected. That's my orders. We've found a few survivors.' More tears fell. 'We saved a boy.'

'Oh, my God! That explains it. A smug colonel came to the processing building and told me not to expect you home for a while. He said you were with a woman, a criminal and drug addict. He looked happy about that.'

'Remember the mission to Yemen?'

'Yes,' she hesitated, finding the sensitive words. 'Where it went wrong, and you were assaulted?'

'Yes. Well, he was a major then. Colonel Winters is his name. He was the officer commanding the Special Forces.'

'Oh.'

'I've had to shoot people, dead.'

'But if there is no cure-'

'They were people once.'

'And your companion?'

'She's been enlisted,' he looked to Imogen. 'Of sorts. She's protecting me. We protect each other. We've found a dog. He's a big bruiser of a German Shepherd. He's killed some of them, too.'

Pippa gave a gasp, which broke Jason's heart, and he wept uncontrollably. He tried to speak, but was racked with sobs.

'Put her on,' she demanded.

Jason reluctantly handed Imogen the phone and continued to weep. He cradled his eyes.

'What's your name?' asked Pippa softly.

'Imogen. Imo.'

'Thank you, Imo, you keep looking out for my husband. Keep him safe.'

'Always.'

'You promise me two things. You find a way through that fence. You bring Jason, unharmed, to me and our baby.'

'I promise,' vowed Imogen, steel in her voice. 'And the other?'

'You put a bullet clean through that smug colonel's forehead.'

'Consider it done,' began Imogen as the line went dead. She looked at the phone, shrugged, and pocketed the mobile. She put her hand through Jason's and gently led him away, back to the Land Rover. He continued to cry uncontrollably, like a small child. Sabre trotting beside them.

Author's Note:

Jason and Imogen will return soon with the next book in The Fence series. I'm having too much fun writing them and I hope you love them as much as me. Isn't Imo naughty!

If you liked this book, it would help me reach new readers if you kindly left a review at Amazon and/or Good Reads. Thank you! This will also help me with a literary contest that I've entered. The judges look at the number of 5-star reviews it receives.

You can follow the progress of my next novel on my social media pages @CGBUSWELL or at www.cgbuswell.com
Join my clan at www.cgbuswell.com/newsletter.php and learn about free books, discounts, and new releases.

Thank you, as always, to my dear friends Ray and Katherine for their advice and eagle-eyed proofreading. If you ever need expert, remote, IT support, Ray can be contacted at www.crudenbaytraining.co.uk or find him in his shop in the village Post Office.

My thanks to Amanda at Let's Get Booked for the stunning cover and diligent formatting. You can see more of her talented book covers at www.letsgetbooked.com

If you've read The Fence and are eagerly awaiting the next book, why not try my short story collection:

Torturous Grief

How far will your grief take you?
Cameron will kill tonight.
It is his duty.

Much blood will be spilt.
He'd stalked his prey for months and will now use his training as a former army nurse.

He'd made a promise. But what is his victim's crime to deserve to be tortured to death? And how long will Cameron use his specialist skills to keep him alive? This box set includes several previously published horror and ghost short stories:

Burnt Vengeance
Christmas at Erskine
Halloween Treat

Reviews for this book:

"What a brilliant short story. I was gripped from beginning to end. I recommend this book. Well done and brilliantly written, as always, Chris."

Available on Amazon

The Drummer Boy

What does the ghost of a 92nd Foot Regiment (The Gordon Highlanders) Drummer Boy want with a modern-day army nurse?

Scott Grey, with his new paranormal psychic abilities, is still haunted by the death of his fiancée. After recuperating on leave in his hometown of Aberdeen, he is stationed in the Garrison Town of Tidworth, where the Napoleonic Wars veteran Drummer Boy's tale of his time at the Battle of Waterloo unfolds.

Will Scott survive this time travel haunting?

5-star reviews for this novel:

"Absolutely brilliant book Chris. So well written. I have no understanding of Wellington or Napoleon, but I understood what was in the book. I feel like I know Scott personally. Would recommend The

Drummer Boy to anyone. Gripping, enthralling, and more. Can't wait for the next adventure."

"Another good read from Chris! The historical research that goes into his stories pays off. I was transported through Scott's eyes to each event that took place. Sad to come to the end, but look forward to the next one. Thank you, Chris."

"Yet again, absolutely BRILLIANT. As expected, another outstanding read from Chris what a brilliant writer he is. Would highly recommend people to read this book as with the first book I felt like I was there with Scott. Please keep writing Chris waiting in anticipation for Scott's next mission. Would have given 10 stars, but it only goes to 5 but well deserves 10."

Available on Amazon

Also, by C.G. Buswell

Novels

The Grey Lady Ghost of the Cambridge Military Hospital: Grey and Scarlet 1
The Drummer Boy: Grey and Scarlet 2
Buried in Grief
One Last War
Group
The Fence

Self Help/Autobiography

Lynne: The Bravehound golden retriever dog who helped me live with my grief and military PTSD

Short Stories

Christmas at Erskine
Halloween Treat
Angelic Gift
Burnt Vengeance
The Release
Christmas Presence
Torturous Grief
Operation Wrath

Printed in Great Britain
by Amazon